The Vengeance Gun

Also by Ray Hogan
in Thorndike Large Print ®

Hell Raiser
Solitude's Lawman
The Bloodrock Valley War
The Renegade Gun
Trouble at Tenkiller

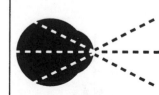

This Large Print Book carries the
Seal of Approval of N.A.V.H.

The Vengeance Gun

Ray Hogan

Thorndike Press • Thorndike, Maine

Library of Congress Cataloging in Publication Data:

Hogan, Ray, 1908-
    The vengeance gun / by Ray Hogan.
        p.   cm.
    ISBN 1-56054-576-3 (alk. paper : lg. print)
    1. Large type books.   I. Title.
[PS3558.O3473V38   1993]   93-21816
813'.54—dc20   CIP

Thorndike Large Print® Western Series edition published
in 1993 by arrangement with Donald MacCampbell, Inc.

Cover design by Peter Nutile.

The tree indicium is a trademark of Thorndike Press.

This book is printed on acid-free, high opacity paper. ∞

Pain roaring through him, Rademacher twisted about. The remaining man should be making his play, assuming there was another. And there had been three gunnies siding Keck in the yard which meant there was still one in front of him to be accounted for. He stiffened, hearing the door of the cabin open. Modesty, her features torn with anxiety, looked down at him.

"Get back," he yelled. "Not over yet!"

Chapter 1

Tom Rademacher drew the dun gelding to a sudden halt as a lean, dark-faced rider broke out of the brush in front of him, effectively blocking the trail. Big hand hovering near the forty-five on his hip, he considered the man coldly.

"What's your problem, mister?"

"Ain't mine, it's yours," the puncher replied, shrugging. "Drifters ain't welcome around here."

"That a fact," Rademacher murmured, glancing about at the wild, rough country. "Just who says so?"

"This here's Joe Keck's range — and he says so. Best you turn around and head back the way you come."

Rademacher smiled gently. "No. I'm going south. Expect I'll keep right on."

The rider's jaw hardened. "You looking for trouble?"

"Nope. Seems I never have to. Always finds me, somehow."

"Well, it's found you again until you do like you're told. Keck don't like strangers riding through this valley."

"He own it?"

"Just about. Reckon he'll have it all before much longer."

"Well, I won't be carrying none of it off. Just passing through."

The rider stiffened. "That mean you ain't turning back?"

"Sure does," Rademacher drawled.

The puncher's hand darted toward the pistol on his hip, froze as Rademacher's gun came up swiftly, leveled at him. His lips tightened and he swallowed noisily.

"I reckon this is your lucky day," Rademacher said. "Ain't often I pull my gun and don't use it. Now, suppose you just cut that horse around and head out over the ridge so's I can move on."

Anger was tearing at the rider's face. For a long breath he stared at Tom Rademacher and then abruptly wheeled about and struck off across the flat crown of the hill immediately ahead.

"Was I you I wouldn't look back for about a mile." The puncher gave no sign of having heard, simply roweled the bay he was riding, and, shoulders stiff, hurried on.

Rademacher holstered his weapon, and, eyes following the man until he was lost to view, moved on toward the summit of the slope up which he had come. A man of dark and sombre mien, he reflected no emotion, neither anger nor amusement, over the incident, seemingly accepting it as a part of living.

Gaining the top of the grade, he again pulled the dun to a stop, and, resting an elbow on the saddle horn, looked out over the valley unrolling below like a vast, undulating green carpet neatly slashed near center by a twisting ribbon of silver. This was the land Joe Keck guarded so jealously; it wasn't hard to see why.

Rademacher let his brooding gaze halt briefly on a scatter of bleak ranch buildings, strangely out of character in the lush country, and then lifted it to the area beyond the valley. Coyote Crossing lay somewhere on to the south. He should reach the settlement by dark according to what he'd been told earlier that day. Tom grunted wearily, glanced at the sun sliding lower in the cloudless arch of a steel blue sky and brushed at the sweat on his forehead. . . . Two or three hours until sunset. He reckoned he'd be there by then.

Another town, another night, another lonely, stuffy room in some two-bit fleabag hotel. He guessed that was to be the history of his life — he who had once had dreams of a fine ranch, a place where he could raise cattle, fine horses, have a family — but was now a footloose, aimless wanderer searching endlessly for a man who seemingly didn't exist but whom yet, he knew, was somewhere.

Pushing his hat to the back of his head, he dropped his glance again to the weathered structures in the near distance. He was still seeing them only vacantly, his bitter thoughts far away. He didn't like to think much on that day five long years in the past — those few violent moments that had changed him and set him adrift, but the time did come now and then and with it that shriveling feeling of emptiness that lately was becoming more and more pronounced.

But he could not quit. Gabe Claunch had to be found — and killed. He'd sworn that on the pine box he'd put Virgil in the day they'd buried him back in the cemetery at Willow Junction. *I'll get him, Virg,* he'd vowed silently as the preacher had intoned a prayer over his brother's body. *I'll hunt him down — kill him — if it takes the rest of my life.*

And well it might. He'd quit his job, taken the several hundred dollars so carefully hoarded for the day when he'd be ready to start up the spread he was planning, and struck out. Gabe Claunch had ridden off fast after shooting down Virgil — seventeen years old, unarmed and posing no threat to him as he came out of the bank after robbing it. It had been by mere chance Virg was standing on the corner opposite; Claunch had cut him down with two bullets and rushed on.

That was five years ago. Five years! Rademacher scrubbed wearily at the whiskers on his jaw. It seemed more like ten, even twenty. Years, months, days that were filled with a desolate sameness; riding, stopping, questions, ranches, towns, the endless plains, deep slashed valleys, and always the results were the same; no one knew Gabe Claunch, no one had ever seen or heard of him.

That was understandable. That Claunch would change his name was certain, even possibly alter his appearance by growing a mustache and beard was to be expected, thus it was a matter of encountering the killer, recognizing him personally, and all that took time and money.

Eventually his original stake had run out. By necessity he had taken a job, staying with it for a time until he had built up sufficient funds to keep him for a few months. Then he would quit, move on, resume the search.

It was a monotonous pattern of life and he fell into the routine, following it almost without conscious awareness. To him it was a means to an end, and as such the hollowness of it was justified. That such a way of life had become habit did not occur to him.

He shifted on the saddle, the ring of brass cartridges in the belt encircling his lean waist glinting dully in the sunlight. A muscular, rawhide sort of man, he looked older than his less than thirty years. His weathered features were quiet, intent, near to morose, a quality that spread also into his eyes and lent them a remoteness that offered little friendliness.

Such was a paradox, however. Beneath the veneer that time with its persisting disappointments had laid upon him there was a loneliness, a need for others. But single-mindedness and solitude builds its own barrier and those outside seldom take the trouble to cross over and find the welcome that lies within.

Motion at the edge of the trees and brush to the east of the ranch buildings tugged at Rademacher's attention. He swung his direct gaze to that point, watched five riders, one on a powerful, white horse, move purposefully onto the hardpack and walk slowly toward the largest of the worn structures.

Tom studied the men briefly, let his glance shift to the buildings. Aged, rag-tag, as destitute looking as the place was, it was some man's home, his private world and the fruits of his labors. *More than I can show for all the years behind me,* he thought bitterly.

The riders halted, the man on the white edging forward a bit from the others. Rademacher frowned. One of the remaining four appeared to be the one who had stopped him on the trail, but another astride a long-legged sorrel drew his frowning attention. There was something familiar about him — the way he sat his saddle, slouched, careless, indifferent to all else.

Tom shaded his eyes with a cupped hand, endeavored to make out the features but the distance was too great. It could be someone he had met before during his travels — and there was a chance the man was Gabe Claunch.

The door of the ranchhouse opened. Two men stepped out, followed by a woman — a young woman judging by the slimness of her shape and bearing. They lined up in front of the riders. The one on the white began to talk, occasionally motioning with a hand.

Rademacher saw the taller of the men who had come from the house shake his head stubbornly. It was some sort of an argument, that was plain, and the weight was all with the riders. . . . A land problem, or perhaps some disagreement over water rights although the stream that coursed through the valley appeared large enough to take care of everyone's needs.

A shout floated up the long slope to Tom, harsh sounding and angry. The word was unintelligible. Suddenly the rider on the white horse drew his pistol. The hills echoed with the blast of the weapon followed by the clatter of broken glass.

The two ranchers went for their weapons. Instantly the warm hush was again broken as more gunshots filled the air. Both men went to their knees, hung briefly and then sprawled full length into the dust as the men siding the one on the white continued to shoot. The faint sound of the girl's scream cut through the fading reports, reached Rademacher.

He heard the leader of the party yell something back at the woman as he wheeled away but whatever it was became lost to him as he roweled the dun and sent him plunging down the grade for the yard.

Chapter 2

Rademacher left his saddle in a long jump and hurried to the girl's side. She was bending over the younger of the two men who was struggling to sit up. Blood soaked the front of his linsey-woolsey gray shirt and one leg of his cord pants. The older man was dead. As he rushed in close the girl whirled, drew back, sudden fear in her eyes.

"Friend," Rademacher said quietly and crouched beside her. He gave the wounded man's injuries brief attention, and slipping his arms under him, came upright.

"This one needs some fixing," he said, looking at the girl. "Afraid there's nothing we can do for the other'n."

She stared at him, stunned despair filling her eyes. "John. . . . dead. I — I know. . . . Rex —"

Rex was the wounded one, the one he was holding, Tom guessed. "Where do you want me to take him?" he pressed gently. "He's bleeding plenty bad."

"I'll be all right," the man muttered weakly. "Expect I can walk."

"Maybe, but you're not trying. Need doctoring."

The words seemed to jar the girl into reality. Rising, she turned, started for the ranchhouse. "Bring him in here."

Entering, she led the way to a bedroom to the left of the doorway. Rademacher laid his burden on the patchwork quilt covering the box-bed and stepped back. The man called Rex looked up at him, pain and shock distorting his features. He was somewhere in his early twenties, huskily built, with bushy, blonde hair.

"Obliged to you," he mumbled. "My brother — you say he's dead?"

Rademacher nodded. Rex made a move to rise. "Got to look after things. . . . Can't expect Modesty —"

"You're in no shape to do anything," Tom said, pressing him back. "Whatever needs doing, I'll do it." He pulled away as the girl crowded by him, added, "You just stay put."

"That's right," she said firmly. "Now, lay still, let me tend those bullet holes."

Rademacher watched her in silence. Rex had called her Modesty and the name fit her well. Evidently she was a younger sister to the two men as there was a strong family resemblance.

After a time she straightened, turned to

Tom. "I don't think he's hurt too bad. . . . I'll show you where to put John — if you will."

Rademacher nodded and followed her back into the main part of the house. She pointed to a second bedroom opening off the same wall.

"In there," she said, her voice breaking suddenly. "My room —"

Tom murmured his understanding, wheeled and returned to the yard. Crossing to where the dead man lay, he took up the body, carried it into Modesty's room and placed it on the bed. He stood for a moment looking down at the stilled features while the memory of a similar moment five long years past flooded through him. It had been his brother then and this like circumstance washed over him in a sudden gust, stirring the sullen embers of hate and fanning the flames of vengeance. He'd find Gabe Claunch and —

Abruptly he turned away from the bed, and, jaw set, crossed to the door. They would need something to bury the man in — a coffin. Stepping out into the yard again, he circled the house and made his way to the barn, absently noting as he did the neglected condition of the place.

It took some scouting around but he finally located the necessary tools, lumber and nails, and for the next hour or so, he bent to the task of putting together a suitable box. Completed, Tom balanced it upon a shoulder, and bringing along the hammer, carried it into the house and placed it on the floor alongside the bed.

Modesty was still with Rex but next to the body of John she had laid out a worn, blue serge suit, a white shirt, celluloid collar, necktie, socks and a worn but polished pair of black shoes. There was also a sheet, snowy white in its cleanness.

Dressing the body, he wrapped it in the sheet and laid it in the coffin after which he stood for a moment in thought. He'd best not nail down the lid yet; it could be the girl and her brother would want a last look at John before the burial.

So deciding, he pulled the pine box into the center room of the house, which served as a parlor, and, setting two chairs at the proper distance apart facing each other, he rested the coffin upon them. The lid he left propped against a nearby wall.

A grave was next in order. Likely there was a family plot somewhere behind the buildings. Going again to the barn he selected a pick and spade from the tools stacked in a corner and headed for a slope a short distance beyond the structures where a small yard enclosed by

18

a picket fence had caught his attention.

There were two round-topped markers; AMOS TODD 1805-1861 had been carved into one of the wooden headboards, PATIENCE TODD 1818-1857 in the other. These were the parents of Modesty and her brothers, Rademacher assumed, and went about the task of digging a third grave in the quiet, matter-of-fact manner that characterized his way.

It was near sundown when he finished, and, standing the tools against a sycamore that shaded the tiny cemetery, he returned to the house, pausing long enough at the pump and horse trough in the yard to wash away the sweat that the physical labor had crusted upon his face, neck and arms.

He found the girl seated beside the coffin, hands clasped in her lap, eyes staring unseeingly through one of the bullet-shattered windows. That she was still stunned by the sudden change in her life was apparent but she glanced around as he entered, managed a wan smile.

"Thank you for all you've done, Mister —"

"Rademacher. Tom Rademacher."

"Mr. Rademacher. . . . I'm Modesty Todd."

He nodded, signifying his knowledge of her and her family. Pointing to the coffin, he said, "It all right there? Didn't know where else to put it but if you want it moved so that friends —"

"Friends?" she cut in with a shrug. "We have none. It's fine where it is."

He considered that for a time. Then, "Grave's dug. One next to your mother. When you're ready I'll carry him out to it."

"Might as well be now — before it's dark."

Rademacher glanced toward the bedroom. "What about your brother? I can bring him in here."

"No need. He said to go ahead without him."

"I see. How is he?"

"As good as I can fix him. Hole in the leg wasn't too hard to doctor. The one in his chest was worse than I thought. I'm not sure about it."

"You want, I'll go fetch a doctor. There's one in Coyote Crossing, I expect."

Modesty nodded. "There is but Rex won't hear of it. Says he'll be all right."

Tom looked closely at her. "You think he will?"

Again her small shoulders stirred. She was much fairer than Rex, he noted, and her eyes were a lighter blue.

"I don't know, but it's what he wants," she replied tonelessly. "If you don't mind putting the lid on the coffin, we can bury John now."

20

Rademacher stepped forward, placed the two boards on the box, and, reaching into a pocket for nails, secured the top while the girl continued to stare out the window.

"It's ready," he said when the chore was done. "It all right if I use that wheelbarrow I saw out back to move him with? Could hitch up your buckboard if you'd rather."

"The wheelbarrow will do."

Obtaining the vehicle, Tom set the coffin across its thick, sturdy sides, and with Modesty steadying it, made the short trip to the burial place. It was difficult lowering the box into the deep trench with only one rope but he succeeded and then drew off to the side, allowing the girl to have her time with her dead.

She stood motionless in the last, golden flare of sunlight, hands folded before her, gaze on the simple pine box coffin while her lips moved slowly in a silent prayer. When she finally stepped back and faced him the first suggestion of tears glittered in her eyes. She had borne up well under her ordeal but now, faced with the reality of the grave, she was nearing the breaking point.

Rademacher started to move forward, lend his comfort and support but she shook her head. "I'll be all right," she murmured.

Taking up the spade Tom completed the

burial, rounding off the mound to match the two adjacent. Done, he brushed at the sweat on his forehead, glanced at Modesty.

"Reckon I ought to be saying it now — didn't get a chance before, but I'm mighty sorry about your brother."

"Thank you," the girl replied in a low voice. "I appreciate your stepping in, doing all you've done — but I guess you're not finished yet."

Tom Rademacher frowned. "What —"

"You might as well dig two more graves — one for Rex and one for me."

Chapter 3

Rademacher stared, nodded slowly. "Figured things was plenty bad, seeing the way that bunch opened up on you and your brothers."

"It's been coming for quite a while but I guess I just really never expected it to happen."

"Natural to always be hoping, I reckon."

"I suppose."

"What's it all about?"

Modesty shook her head. "I don't want to burden you with our troubles —"

"Sort of used to it, and I expect it'd do you some good to talk about it."

The girl smiled hesitantly. "Well, if you want to listen let's go back to the house. There's coffee on the stove."

Leaving the wheelbarrow with the tools in it at the barn, Tom followed Modesty across the hardpack and into the kitchen. As he settled onto one of the straight backed chairs placed around a small table, Rex called from the bedroom.

"It over with?"

"He's buried," Modesty answered, taking

cups from the cabinet built into the wall. "Next to Ma."

Filling the chipped china containers from the enameled pot simmering on the stove, she set them on the table and sat down opposite Rademacher wearily.

"I'll thank you again for helping," she murmured. "Don't know what I would have done if you hadn't come along when you did."

"You'd've managed. Folks always do, somehow."

He studied her over the rim of his cup. Her face was calm, resigned and there was a heaviness filling her eyes. Modesty was more than just an attractive woman, he saw, one actually pretty.

"This trouble," he prompted softly, "it over your land?"

She looked up wondering. "How'd you know?"

His wide shoulders lifted and fell. "Out in this part of the country it's usually somebody wanting more range or water that starts things boiling — and it looks to me like that river's big enough to take care of everybody."

"It's the land, all right — this place. Joe Keck wants it."

"Keck. . . . Name's been mentioned to me. He the one on the white horse?"

"That's him. Where did you hear of him?"

"Fellow stopped me back on the other side of the ridge. Said Keck didn't like nobody riding across his property, told me to turn back."

A faint smile tugged at the corners of Modesty's lips. "But you didn't."

"Nope. I was pointing south and there wasn't no good reason to head back the other way. Had to sort of convince the fellow, then he rode off. Saw him later in that bunch that was with this Keck."

"You weren't on Crosshatch land," Modesty said. "He had no right to order you off. Place is still ours."

"Must need it mighty bad to go after it the way he is."

"Don't need it at all!" Rex shouted from the bedroom. "Owns more range now than he can use — it's just that he's got a bug to own the whole valley."

Rademacher took up the pot of coffee, refilled his cup. Modesty had barely touched hers. "What about the law? Can't you get some help from —"

"The law!" Rex echoed scornfully. "All we've got around here is a deputy and he same as works for Keck. Could say he's just another Crosshatch hired-hand."

Modesty rose, walked to where her brother

lay. "I want you to quiet down. You're getting all upset again and you need rest. You're not doing yourself any good."

"Not doing a damned bit of good on this bed, either," he snapped impatiently.

"You'll be doing those wounds some good. Try to sleep."

Rex mumbled a reply and Modesty said something in an equally low voice to him. Then, returning to the table, she resumed her chair.

"This Keck been around long?" Tom asked.

"Always — or so it seems. Henry Keck, he was Joe's pa, started the Crosshatch Ranch. Built it into the biggest place in the valley and did it without hurting anybody. He died about a year ago and Joe took over."

"That when the trouble began?"

The girl nodded. "He started taking over all the other ranches, buying them out — usually at his own price. When folks wouldn't sell he made it hard on them until they changed their minds and gave in."

"He's gone plumb crazy!" Rex declared, coming back into the conversation. "Aims to get the whole valley any way he can. Hired himself a bunch of hardcases to back his play. Ain't nobody been able to buck him except us and you can see where it's got us — but we ain't quitting — not yet, not long as I can use a gun!"

"You can't fight them alone, Rex," Modesty said lifelessly.

"Maybe I can't but I sure as hell will!" he shot back angrily. "Place is ours. Belonged to us from the day pa homesteaded it and the only way Joe Keck'll get it is over my dead body!"

"John said that, too, and now he's in his grave."

There was a long silence after that and then Rex said: "You want to give in, lose what little we've got?"

"No, only I don't see how —"

"Settles it. We'll fight for what's ours. I'll get help — hire some gunslingers —"

"That'll take money, Rex," Modesty said, sighing. "A lot of money."

"I'll get it," Todd vowed in a falling voice. "I'll find a way."

Tom Rademacher listened quietly, his own problems forgotten momentarily in the shadow of someone else's trouble.

"You the only ones left Keck hasn't run off? Was thinking you could get the other ranchers that are having the same fight with him together and make a stand."

"Too late now — we're the last hold-out. Besides, we tried that. John called a meeting when it first started. There were a few who agreed to not sell to him but they changed. Keck and his crowd were too much for them — too ruthless."

"What about the town? Can't you get help from the merchants?"

"They do what Keck wants. He's their biggest customer now that most everyone else is gone. They won't oppose him but do just what he tells them to do the same as the deputy."

"Deputy's not the only law in the Territory. How about the U.S. Marshal?"

"It wouldn't do any good to write him. He'd not be interested in our problem — not wanting to sell out, I mean. And far as John's death is concerned, Keck would claim it was self-defense, that John and Rex drew their guns on him. . . . I guess that's what happened, in a way. When Joe started shooting out the windows, they meant to stop him. Then the rest of the bunch began firing."

"He's a smart one for sure," Rademacher admitted. "Keeps himself plenty well covered. Heard him yell something at you when they rode out, couldn't make out what it was he said."

"Told me that was only a sample of what would happen now if we didn't sell to him, and that he'd be back for his answer."

Abruptly Modesty turned away as a sob wrenched her. "Oh, it's been like a nightmare — a terrible nightmare! Why does it have to be us?"

"You're not the first," Tom said. "Know that's not much comfort but it's the truth. Happens right along. World's full of the Joe Kecks out to take what they want any way they can. I've seen a lot of it."

"It's wrong —"

"Is for a fact, and folks don't have much luck fighting them. Man gets big and powerful, he can get away with about whatever he wants especially out here in this part of the country where the law hasn't got around to working good yet."

"Law! There is no law for people like us!"

"We're making our own law!" Rex called from the bedroom. "Nobody helps us. Leaves us with the chore of looking out for ourselves — and that's what I aim to keep on doing."

Modesty came around slowly, eyes searching Tom Rademacher's sun and wind browned face. "What do you think we ought to do? Fight, hold on to what's ours, or give in to Joe Keck, take what he's willing to pay for the place and move on?"

Rademacher stirred restlessly under the direct question as he toyed with his empty cup. Somewhere in the trees behind the house a dove mourned dolefully into the closing darkness.

"Hard for me to answer that, considering the way things stand, and I've got an idea of what your ranch means to you. But I know the kind this Joe Keck is and I don't figure you can win against him. He's holding all the good cards."

"Then you think we ought to quit — give in."

"A shame but you asked and I'm being honest. Keck won't hold back none because you're a woman and your brother sure is in no shape to put up a fight. Way I see it now you ain't got a prayer."

"But — to lose everything, all we've worked for —"

"You said he was willing to pay something for the place. Might be enough to go somewhere else, start up another ranch. I reckon that's better than dying."

"No!"

The word exploded into the room. Modesty and Tom turned about in surprise. Rex, bandages showing freshly red, had risen from the bed, was leaning weakly against the door frame.

"Joe Keck'll have to kill me to get me off my land!"

Chapter 4

Modesty came from her chair, hurried across the room to her brother. Rademacher rose, moved to her side.

"Best you take it easy," he said soothingly, taking the injured man by the arm. "You're in no shape to be on your feet."

Todd jerked away, shook his head violently. "Can still fight for what's mine — die for it, too, if need be."

"What about your sister? You aim to drag her down, too?"

Steadying himself, Rex looked at the girl. "Up to her," he mumbled. "Not telling her she has to stay with me. Not even asking her. Only saying what I've got to do."

Modesty, taking over, gripped his arm, and turning him around, guided him back to the bed. "We'll talk about it later," she said. "After you've rested. I'll fix some supper. Once you've had something to eat you'll feel stronger."

Rademacher swung back to the table. Darkness was closing in, and, striking a match, he lit the lamps. From the bedroom he heard

31

Rex Todd call out.

"How about you? Looking for work?"

"Nope," Tom answered, "I'm on the move. Headed for town — Coyote Springs. I don't find who I'm hunting for there, I keep heading south."

"It real important?"

"To me," Rademacher said and then paused, remembering the man in Keck's party who looked familiar. "That bunch with Joe Keck, you know them all?"

Modesty reappeared, worry pulling at her features. She made a warning gesture with a hand, said, "He's resting again. Maybe if we don't talk loud —"

Tom nodded as she moved on by him to the stove. Halting there Modesty quietly began preparations for the evening meal.

"You'll eat with us, of course," the girl said in a low voice. "Those men — you asked if we knew them all. We do. They've all been here before several times. Why?"

"Was one a big fellow riding a sorrel horse. Thought I might have had some dealings with him."

Modesty paused in the act of peeling potatoes. "On a sorrel," she repeated, and bobbed her head. "That's Pete Webber. He's been at Crosshatch for quite a time. Keck's top gunhand, I've heard John say."

Webber — that was a long way from Claunch, but a man could change his name — and that's what he expected the killer to do. "What about the others?"

"Well, there's one named Sackett. He was the redhead. And Enos Hatton, the tall, skinny one with real light eyes. Last one was Lon Phillips."

"He the one riding the bay?"

Modesty had paused, a sort of stillness coming over her. The thought came to Tom that at one time there must have been something between the girl and Phillips, something that became lost or was destroyed by the trouble that had crept into the valley.

"Yes — why?"

"He's the one that tried to stop me on the ridge."

She gave that a few moments' thought and then shrugged, continued her chore. "Lon used to own a ranch west of us. We were — well — good friends, but he sold out to Keck and went to work for him."

Likely they had been more than just good friends, Rademacher decided but he did not press the idea. If she wanted to tell him more, she would.

"Do you know any of them?" Modesty asked, letting the subject drop.

"The names don't stir my mind none. Still

figure I ought to know that one on the sorrell, however — Webber, you said he was called."

"Probably not his real name. Most of the kind who go to work for Joe Keck are outlaws, hiding from something or someone." She turned to Tom suddenly. "You say you were looking for somebody?"

"Man name of Gabe Claunch. He killed my brother."

A stillness came over the girl again. "And now you're out to kill him —"

"About the way it stacks up."

Sighing, she dumped the thinly-sliced potatoes into a skillet, already crackling with hot grease. "I thought it would be something like that — the way you act and that grim sort of look you have. How long have you been hunting this Claunch?"

"Five years, thereabouts."

She turned to him in astonishment. "Five years! Why, he could be dead by now!"

"Maybe, only I don't know that, and I've got to be sure."

Modesty studied him closely, her eyes frank and wondering. "After all that time, it still means so much to you seeing him dead?"

Rademacher nodded, vaguely uncomfortable under her direct gaze. "You're needing more firewood, I figure. I'll fetch it."

Wheeling, he opened the back door and

stepped out into the warm darkness of the night. It was pleasant and he stood for a time enjoying the soft hush while the wonder in the girl's tone at his determination to find Claunch after so long a time pricked at his mind.

Abruptly he shrugged it off. What did she expect? That he should give up, forget it, let Gabe Claunch get away with the cold-blooded murder of Virgil? What the hell did time have to do with it? Virg was dead forever; why shouldn't he search until he found his killer — even if it took a lifetime?

Crossing to the woodpile, Tom gathered up an armload of the split sticks and carried them back into the house. The stove was adding to the warmness of the night and he left the door open, permitting a faint breeze to enter.

Modesty had placed meat in a second spider and the room was beginning to fill with the good sound and smell of frying food. Unloading the wood in the box set nearby for such purpose, he crossed to the room where Rex Todd lay and glanced in. The man was on his back, sleeping restlessly. Tom studied him briefly, noting the ruddiness of his face, the twitching of his mouth, and returned to where Modesty was slicing thick chunks from a loaf of bread.

"Don't aim to be adding to your trouble but your brother's going to need a doctor. I don't think he's doing much good."

Alarm filled the girl's eyes, and laying aside the bread knife, she hurried to the bedroom. After a bit she reappeared.

"He does feel feverish," she said worriedly, "but he still refuses to let me get Doctor Ross."

"Maybe you'd better not listen to him. Wait until morning. If he's no better then, do it anyway."

"Will it be all right to hold off that long?"

"Probably. What he's needing is sleep and rest, and some good, hot grub when he wakes up. Could be better by sunrise."

Modesty resumed her task at the stove. "Will you stay here tonight?" she asked, hesitantly.

He gave that thought, found the idea of leaving the girl alone and helpless with her injured brother not to his liking, but he expressed it in a different way.

"Was aiming to camp somewhere close by, wait for Keck and his bunch to show up again. Want a close-up look at that one who calls himself Webber. Could be he's the man I'm hunting for."

Relief flooded Modesty's drawn features. "Oh, I'm so glad!" she cried. "I don't know when they'll come again — maybe tonight, and with Rex hurt, I —" She brushed at her eyes. "I've never been afraid before, but seeing them shoot down John —"

Rademacher reached out, took her by the shoulders and drew her close, comforting her as best he could. She wept quietly against him for a bit, and then, regaining composure, drew back.

"I — I had better get supper ready," she said, producing a small smile. "You're probably about starved. . . . As for camping somewhere, you'll do no such thing! You can stay in the cabin."

"Cabin?"

"It's our old house, the one we lived in before pa and my brothers built this one. We left it standing, planned to use it for the hired-hands when we got the ranch built up to where we needed a crew."

"Don't want to put you out any."

"You won't be. The place hasn't been used in years and it still has some of our old furniture in it. You can move right in. Why don't you do that now? Put your horse in the barn with ours — you'll find feed for him. By the time you're finished, we'll be ready to eat."

Tom smiled, turned to the door. Sleeping inside, on a bed would be a nice change from rolling up in a blanket out in the hills somewhere — and he would be on hand when Webber showed himself again. Of course, he could easily ride over to Keck's Crosshatch Ranch and look the man up, or, chances were, he would encounter him in town.

Waiting here at the Todd place seemed a much better idea, however.

Chapter 5

There were five horses in the barn Tom noticed after he had struck a match to the lantern he found hanging just inside the door. Leading the dun into an empty stall, he stripped the big gelding of gear and provided him with a quantity of feed. That done, he took up his saddlebags and blanket roll and turned for the exit.

Apparently the Todds were down to minimums insofar as stock was concerned; likely their herd of cattle consisted of only a few hundred head, if that many, if he could judge by their other possessions. All in all, and taking the ranch as a whole into consideration, Modesty and Rex had little to lose by selling out to Joe Keck other than the fact of losing the family holdings; that was what counted with them, he guessed, and then, smiling ruefully, told himself that such, however valueless, was more than he could show for a lifetime.

Stepping out onto the hardpack, he crossed to the smaller house a short distance away. Full night had settled over the land, and entering the pitch-dark structure he paused, lit a match and glanced around for a lamp. There was one on a nearby table but it was empty of oil, and leaving his gear, retraced his steps to the barn where he refilled the lamp's reservoir from a five gallon can he had noted earlier.

The cabin he saw, once the light was spreading through it, had three small bedrooms that lay off a single, large area serving as parlor, kitchen and dining quarters. The place was tight and comfortable, and, dropping his possessions onto the first bed handy, he sat down beside them to do a bit of thinking.

It was foolish to mix himself in someone else's trouble and by so doing he was breaking a rule he'd assiduously observed for years; he'd be smart to load up right then and ride on. The squabble between the Todds and Joe Keck was their own and would resolve itself eventually, one way or another — likely the way Keck wanted. And there could be two sides to the story.

Such matters often went far back, had their roots in incidents that involved the parents or even grandparents of those now engaged in controversy. It could be that Keck had good cause for wanting to take over the Todd holdings. Rademacher had to admit that it was possible just as there might be a reason for the man's ruthlessness but he had his doubts as to that; to make war on a family that consisted of a girl and two men with a gang of hardcase gunslingers hardly denoted a man being in the right.

Still, it was no business of his. He'd seen like situations many times and almost always the victory had gone to the strong — just as he'd told Modesty. Fighting someone like Keck was a hopeless proposition with no more strength than they had to show.

He found himself in sympathy with them, nevertheless, and the fact that he was staying over the night was an indication of concern, however reluctant.

Rising, he dug into his saddlebags for a towel and a clean shirt, and obtaining a bucket of water from the pump, he scrubbed himself clean and pulled on the fresh garment. He saw Modesty silhouetted in the doorway of the kitchen shortly after that. She was beckoning to him, and after brushing his hair into place with the palms of his hands, he hurried to heed her summons.

It was a fine supper, the mood of it dampened of course by the death and burial of John Todd, but he enjoyed every moment of it. Sitting across from the quiet-faced girl, eating the tasty food, he was almost happy that her brother Rex slept and they could be alone.

41

He had missed all this, Rademacher realized as he relaxed with a final cup of coffee while Modesty cleared the table. The years had slipped away, passing him completely, leaving him with only memories of long, empty nights, hot or perhaps cold days and trails that led to nowhere. A man deserved more than that — but a man also must live up to his obligations and until he had discharged the one that rode his shoulders, he could hope for little else.

"Is the cabin all right?" the girl asked when her chores were done and she had settled again in her chair.

"Fine. Sure going to appreciate that bed. Sleeping on the ground gets a mite old after a time."

"We had hoped to fix it up before now. Had a good start towards doing it when we lost out."

"Lost out?"

"There was a blizzard. Four years back. We had a dry summer and then a bad winter. It snowed for several days and after that there came a hard freeze. We lost over half our herd."

"Seems I remember hearing about that storm. How many head are you running now?"

"Only three hundred or so. It's been a struggle to get back on our feet — and now with Keck —"

The words trailed off as her voice faltered. She glanced involuntarily through the open door to the yard beyond as if half expecting the rancher to appear. Tom reached into a pocket for tobacco and papers, rolled himself a smoke. Faint mutterings were coming from the bedroom where Rex Todd lay. There was no change in the man, he guessed.

"I wish you could stay on," she continued after a time. "You could live in the cabin, work for us, like Rex said. I've been thinking about it. We could sell off a few steers to pay you whatever you'd charge."

Rademacher shifted on his chair. "Mighty hard to turn down the offer, but —"

"Rex and I would both be grateful. . . . And I'd like it very much."

He gave that thought, shrugged. "Reckon I would, too, only —"

"You've got to find the man who killed your brother," she finished wearily. "I wish I could understand why it's so important to you."

"Keck shot down your brother, almost killed Rex; doesn't that bother you?"

"Of course, but it's something that will take care of itself without me turning my life into a search for vengeance. Keck will have to account for what he did someday."

"Account to who?"

"Some other man, probably. One who will shoot faster and straighter than him or the men he hires."

"I can't wait for that to happen to Gabe Claunch."

"Why not? Why waste your life hunting for somebody that you're not even sure is still alive?"

"Because I have to, I reckon. Said I would. Swore it on the body of my brother. Can't quit until I've seen it through."

"Vengeance and hate — they've ruined many a life," Modesty said. "And they're ruining yours. I wish I could make you see that."

"All I can see is Virgil laying dead in the street and the man who shot him riding off — free. Some difference in what happened to your brother. He was a man grown and he had a gun. Virg was only a boy and he didn't have a weapon."

"Dead is dead just the same and nothing you can ever do will change that. . . . Will you be riding on in the morning after you see if Webber is the man you're looking for?"

"What I figured on. Going first to town. Can drop by the doc's if you want."

"Rex seems no better or no worse. Morning could bring a change, as you said. I'll know

44

by then," Modesty answered, rising, bringing Rademacher to his feet also.

"Probably you're wanting to turn in," he said. "Can use a little shut-eye myself. . . . Want to thank you again for the supper. Was a fine meal."

"Only right after what you did for us," the girl replied listlessly. "Good night."

"Night," Tom said, and moved out into the starlit night. He walked slowly across the yard to the cabin still thinking of the words Modesty had spoken, wondering, too, at the fact he'd found it necessary to defend his way of life. A man must do what he thought right, and tracking down Gabe Claunch, exacting payment from him for what he had done was necessary and expected. He couldn't have been wrong believing that for all those years.

Or could he?

Disturbed, he stood for a time in the doorway of the cabin smoking one cigarette after another while he stared off into the pale, silvered night and pondered the question. He could find no answer and, finally giving up, turned into the bedroom and, throwing himself on the corn-shuck mattress, dropped off to sleep.

Chapter 6

Rademacher was awake early. He lay for a time, luxuriating in the comfort of a real bed, listening to birds singing in the nearby trees, the homey clucking of chickens in their yard, and then finally rolled out. Dressing hurriedly, he dug out his razor and soap, did a fair job of scraping off the whiskery stubble on his face. That completed, he pulled on his hat, and strapping on his six-gun, stepped out into the yard.

The morning was warm and quiet with the sun just beginning to push above the rolling horizon to the east. The land beyond the Todd place looked green and soft with grass tassles stirring only slightly, and the trees ringing the yard were thick with leaves. Evidently the valley had enjoyed a wet spring. He glanced toward the house. He could see no indication that Modesty was up and about yet, and moving on, crossed the hardpack to the fenced off garden he could see beyond its edge.

It was well kept, showed signs of having been weeded only recently. Corn, squash, potatoes, beans, melons, rows of onions and other vegetables, it undoubtedly provided the Todds with all they desired in green fare. On its yonder side were several fruit trees, all heavily burdened. Chickens, a few hogs and a milk cow occupied pens adjacent to the barn, while on the flat farther to the west fields of hay and alfalfa were doing well.

Living was complete on the Todd holdings. Tom could see that. With both meat and produce of their own they had little need to depend on the outside world except for those few necessities that could not be grown. . . . That was the way it should be, he thought; a man ought to be wholly independent, not rely on others for anything — and in that observation he had a better understanding why the Todds, against such great odds, were willing to fight to hold their property.

Moving on, he wandered aimlessly toward the rear of the structures, noting the unused corrals, the sagging sheds. Crossing behind the hulking barn, he reached the opposite side. Under a canopied shelter he saw a buckboard, a two-seated buggy, a light spring wagon. Harness, well back in out of the weather, hung from pegs on the wall.

Here, in contrast to the garden and livestock, all appeared unused, and it came to him that the Todds were being compelled to neglect the cattle raising end of their ranch, that they were virtually prisoners of Joe Keck and his men, unable to do much other than stay close to the ranchhouse and its companion structures while all else went begging.

It was a damned shame. The place could do well, and with a few good breaks might be built up into a fine, beef raising ranch if it wasn't for Keck.

Modesty's woodpile looked small and in need of replenishing. Crossing to it, he took up the double-bit ax and started to work on the row of stacked logs, splitting them first into quarters and then chopping them to stove length. He was hard at the chore when she called him in to a breakfast of bacon, eggs, hot biscuits, honey and coffee.

He ate with relish but not unaware of the tension and worry that gripped the girl but again he made no probing comment, left it for her to break the silence when she was ready. It came after he finished the meal.

"I don't think Rex is any better," she said in a heavy voice. "Worse, if anything."

Rademacher was a bit surprised; he thought it was the impending return of Keck and his hardcase riders that caused her concern. Admiration stirred through him, and rising, he went into the bedroom. Todd was asleep. His face was flushed, his skin hot to the touch.

Fever had unquestionably set in.

"Like it or not, we're getting the doctor," Tom said, returning to the kitchen. "If he hollers about it, let him."

Modesty was looking at him intently, a faint smile now on her lips at his plural decisiveness. After a moment he grinned self-consciously.

"I mean if you want to," he amended.

She was serious instantly. "I do. Dr. Ross is the only one in town so you won't have any trouble finding him."

"I'll ride in soon as Keck shows up, if that's all right with you. Little surprised he hasn't come by now — or even last night."

"Never know what he'll do. It might be tomorrow for all I know. I think he does it that way just to worry us more."

"Probably. Could go now only I don't like leaving you alone, but I reckon we oughtn't to hold off too long."

"No. If he hasn't come by the middle of the morning, you should go anyway."

"Don't like taking the chance —"

"Everything's been a chance lately. If you do, what about Webber?"

"No problem. I can look him up at Keck's ranch or maybe I'll run into him in town."

Modesty looked away. "Then, if you do that you won't be back."

Rademacher did not answer, only shrugged.

The silence ran on for a time. Finally, "What do you figure to tell Keck when he shows up?"

She made a small gesture with her hands, shook her head. "I don't know. I feel the same as Rex — that we can't give in. But with John gone —"

Modesty had changed her dress, he saw, now wore a simple blue and white affair that brought out the good points of her figure. Her hair, too, was arranged different, having been pulled in close to frame her face.

"Wish there was some way I could help."

"I understand, and you think it's hopeless anyway, useless to fight. I suppose you're right but maybe, never having had your own place, a home that your parents worked and struggled to build and leave for you, you don't really feel as we do."

"I gave up my idea of that when Virg was killed," Tom said quietly. "Had sweated and saved for a long time so's I could have a ranch of my own. Claunch put an end to it."

"I'm sorry," she said contritely. "I just supposed you started out hunting him, never thought that you had to give up something you wanted."

"Times when things like that don't seem important."

"I know, and I've tried to convince myself that Rex and I are faced with that now. I studied about it all night but the answer came out the same every time. Keeping our place is important to us. It means our family, what they did on this earth, all the work and hope and faith they put into it. I can't just turn my back on all of that."

"Reckon I savvy your feelings a little better now than I did. Sort of looked things over this morning. It's a fine ranch, one you've a right to be proud of and one you could turn into a big spread, given a bit of luck. Expect I was shooting off my mouth last night when I said what I did."

"About giving up without a fight? No, you made sense. It's the only practical thing to do, only I guess Rex and I aren't sensible when it comes down to that. Neither was John, for that matter — thinking we could stand up against Joe Keck. . . . But that's the way it'll have to be."

Rademacher looked at the girl sharply. "That mean you've made up your mind to buck him?"

She nodded. "Just how, with Rex hurt, I don't know. When Keck sees that there's only me left to fight he'll maybe draw off and let us alone until Rex is on his feet again. That will give me — us time to get some help, hire several men."

Tom Rademacher said nothing but in his

mind was the conviction that such would mean little to Joe Keck; that he had only a slip of a girl to deal with would to him be considered a distinct advantage, one to be capitalized on immediately. The Kecks of the world got where they were by grasping such opportunities.

"Still figure you'd be smart to get word to the U.S. Marshal, tell him what's going on. Maybe wouldn't do much for you personally but he just might straighten that deputy out. And there's been a killing. No matter how it happened the law always wants to know what it was all about — leastwise that's the way of it every place I've been."

"I could write a letter, I suppose, mail it to him at the capital. Maybe he could —"

Modesty's words broke off. A tautness came over her features as she looked beyond him, through the open doorway into the yard.

Rademacher's eyes narrowed. "Keck?"

She moved her head slightly. "He's come," she said.

Chapter 7

Rademacher wheeled to the doorway and glanced out. Keck, again on his white horse, had halted with three riders at the edge of the yard. He appeared to be looking over the place as if considering what he could do with it, once his.

Pete Webber was not in the party. Tom swore softly. He had counted on having his close inspection of the man and determine if he was Gabe Claunch or not. Now it would have to wait for another time.

Keck jerked his head at his followers and moved in. He was a man in his early thirties, Tom reckoned, big boned, thick shouldered, and with a dark, tough way about him.

"You — Todds!"

At the rancher's harsh summons Rademacher glanced at Modesty. She had paled and there was a glint of fear in her eyes. He nodded, smiled tightly.

"Just keep remembering — he's only a man, same as others. Don't let him buffalo you."

The girl swallowed, and visibly gathering her courage, stepped out into the yard. Tom, hitching his gun forward, closed in behind her. Once in the open, he took up a stand a few paces to her left.

At once Joe Keck straightened. Phillips kneed his bay mount in beside him, said something. The rancher nodded and made a reply that included all of the riders. Immediately they spread out into a line little more than a stride apart. Rademacher studied them coldly; none of them, other than Lon Phillips, was familiar, and certainly Gabe Claunch was not among the party.

Keck, glaring at Modesty, pointed a long finger at Rademacher. "Who's he?"

"A friend," she replied evenly.

The rancher swept Tom again with his glance, touching him from weather-stained hat to worn boots as he made his assessment. Again he said something in a low voice to his men. All nodded briefly to signify their understanding.

"Well, what's it to be?" he demanded, turning to Modesty once more. "I want to hear it — now."

The girl's shoulders came up. "The answer's the same as before."

"And it ain't never going to be no different!"

Rademacher swung in exasperation to the door. Rex Todd had again left his bed, now stood braced in the opening, hair disheveled, eyes bright with fever. Tom looked hurriedly at the man's hand, sighed in relief; he was not holding a weapon. Had he been trouble would have erupted quickly.

"Rex — you shouldn't —" Modesty began and started toward him anxiously.

Todd waved her back. "I'm all right. I can talk and say what needs saying." He shifted his burning gaze to the rancher. "Telling you for the last time, we ain't selling out. Now, take your hired-hands and get off our property!"

Keck settled back on his saddle, wagged his head. "Figured you'd learned your lesson by now, Rex."

Todd raised an arm angrily, abruptly sagged against the door frame. "You —" he began, and fell silent.

Modesty turned fiercely upon the rancher. "Haven't you done enough to us?" she cried. "You've — you've killed John, and maybe Rex, too! Can't you leave us alone now?"

Keck smiled. "No, ma'am," he said in mock politeness. "Sure can't, not until you've moved off this land. Now, you pack up and pull out, then it'll be different. Won't ever be me or any of my boys bothering you again."

"No —" Rex shouted in a strangled voice. "We won't ever leave!"

"That what you say, lady?" Keck asked.

Modesty nodded. "You can't drive us off. . . . Never."

"A long time, never."

"I mean it. This is our place, our land and you can't take it away from us. We'll go to the law, to the U.S. Marshal!"

"What good'll that do? He takes one look at this starved-out cabbage patch and he'll know same as everybody else that you ought to sell. He'll be sure of it when he finds out that it's me offering to buy. Big place like mine means something to the Territory. Why don't you use a little horse sense?"

"Wasting your breath, Heck," Rex called in a labored tone. "Nothing will make us give up. You just as well quit talking."

"Once I do you'll be wishing it was the other way," the rancher snapped. "I've gone easy on you, your old man and my pa having been friends the way they were, but I'm getting tired of dilly-dallying. Aim to wind this thing up. Got other fish to fry."

"Then you best get at it because we ain't changing our minds."

"Maybe you will," Keck said and glanced at the rider immediately on his right. "Ike, you and Amos trot around back, see if that old barn'll burn like I figure. Being dry as gunpowder it ought —"

"Forget it!" Rademacher barked, letting his arms fall to his sides. "You've got your answer, and you've been told to get off the place. Be smart and do it."

The two men halted uncertainly. Keck stared coldly at Tom. "You cutting yourself in on this deal, mister?"

"Reckon so."

"Could be you're biting off more'n you can chew. Who the hell are you?"

"Don't see that it matters but the name's Rademacher. I'm a friend of the family, like Miss Todd says."

"And bucking for the graveyard if you start getting in my way."

"Ain't we all," Tom drawled. "Giving you a little advice; turn that stud around and get out of here before things grow any worse."

Keck frowned, glanced at his men, then swiveled his attention back to Modesty. "A hired gun ain't going to do you no good, lady. I've got a dozen of them, some the best in the business. Best you call off this jasper before you have to bury him, too."

Modesty stirred uncertainly. Rademacher did not take his eyes off the rancher and his riders. Such a thoughtless move could cost him his life.

"You need telling again?"

Keck studied Tom thoughtfully. He seemed

57

puzzled, almost as if he found the moment hard to believe. "You sure you know what you're doing?"

"Sure do."

"You figure you've got a chance against the four of us?"

"Considering what I'm facing, I've seen worse odds."

Keck bristled. "What's that mean?"

"Never saw a man yet big at pushing a woman around that had much sand for anything else."

"The hell! It's her that's making this happen. I've been dealing with them brothers of hers and there wasn't no backing down by me."

"Not hard when you've got five guns standing behind you."

The rancher shrugged. "What I pay them for. Anyways, the Todds hadn't ought've drawn on me."

"Had the right. Were protecting their property. The law'll probably give you the horse laugh if you go claiming self-defense."

"The law knows which side of the bread the butter's on," Keck said, smiling thinly.

"Not talking about that deputy. I figure the Todds ought to do their talking to somebody higher up."

"And I figure talking's all you aim to do,"

Joe Keck yelled and jerked his head at the men beside him. "Get at it, boys!"

Rademacher's weapon came into his hand in a single, swift blur. It rapped sharply through the warm, morning hush. Dirt spurted in front of the riders, sprayed the hooves of their horses, sent them shying off. Keck swore wildly as the stallion he rode began to rear.

Tom waited until the confusion ended, and then, pistol leveled at the rancher's belly, smiled drily.

"Best you do your figuring over, friend. I've got four bullets left in this iron. First one's yours."

Chapter 8

Keck, anger twisting his features, filling his eyes with a hard glitter, stared at Rademacher.

"Damn you!" he yelled. "Who the hell do you think you are?"

"I'm the one leveling down on you," Tom said blandly.

"You can't hold off four guns —"

"Maybe not," Rademacher cut in, "but if your bunch opens up on me, my first slug's going into you. We'll make that trip to hell together."

The rancher stirred nervously, glanced at the men siding him. "You're loco if you think you can buck me," he said. "Maybe you're fast with that forty-five but I've got a couple of hired-hands that can take you any time I give the word."

"One of them called himself Pete Webber? Sure would like to meet him."

"More'n likely you will," Keck said in a promising sort of way. "Horning in like this is liable to cost you your hide."

"I'll take my chances," Tom replied coolly.

"Now, like you've already been told, take your outfit and get off the property — and stay off."

Keck bobbed his head curtly. "We're going, but we'll be back — and you and them Todds better not be here when we do!"

Sawing savagely at the reins, the rancher wheeled the white about, and raking the stallion with his spurs, led his men out of the yard.

Rademacher drew a deep breath. "Close," he murmured, punching out the empty cartridge in the cylinder of his pistol and reloading. "Plenty close."

In the next moment he heard a thump and a cry of alarm from Modesty. He pivoted, saw the girl running for the house. Rex lay half in and half out of the doorway.

Tom caught up to her in a half a dozen long strides. Reaching Todd, he slipped his arms under the suffering man, lifted him, and carrying him back into the house, laid him on the bed. Rex groaned deeply.

"They gone?"

Modesty, her face chalk white as she set about replacing the bandages, freshly soaked from his efforts, nodded.

"But they'll be back," she said in a worn tone. "Rex, you've got to stop getting up.

You break those wounds open every time you do —"

"I'm doing fine," Todd replied impatiently.

"All you're doing is killing yourself and making things worse," Rademacher snapped.

"Can't just lay here. Cattle needs tending to — and I got to get set for Keck and his bunch —"

"Only thing you've got to do is stay put in that bed until you're well again. I'll look after your chores. . . . And Keck."

Todd frowned, focused his eyes on Tom. "That mean you're sticking around — hiring on?"

"Ain't had my look at this Pete Webber yet," he said, shrugging. "Figure to hold off 'til I do."

The injured man relaxed visibly. "Mighty glad to hear that, no matter why you're doing it. Expect you don't know it but you're the first man that's ever stood up to Joe Keck and his hired gunnies and come out on top."

"About time, I'd say," Tom murmured and backed toward the doorway. "Get yourself some rest, else I might go changing my mind and ride on."

Todd mustered a grin. "Sure, sure."

"I still think we ought to get Dr. Ross," Modesty said, finishing her work. "Wounds don't look good at all."

"Hurt like all get-out, too," Rex agreed, "but I expect that's my fault. Don't be worrying so now, however. I'll be all right."

"We need some real medicine —"

"I'll make you a deal, sis," Rex interrupted, laying his hand on the girl's arm. "If I ain't plenty better by tomorrow morning, you can send for Ross. That suit you?"

Modesty, lips tightly compressed, shrugged in assent, and, turning, closed the connecting door and joined Rademacher in the main room of the house. He had helped himself to a cup of coffee, now stood watching her as she moved up to him.

"I don't want you to stay."

He stared at her in amazement, searching her strained features for an explanation to the change in her thinking.

"Why not?" he asked, finally.

"There's no reason for you to mix yourself up in our troubles. We were wrong to ask — and you can't fight them alone."

"Not all at the same time," he said, grinning.

Modesty shook her head. "Don't try to make light of it — and you're not fooling me by claiming you're staying so's you can get a look at Pete Webber. You could go find him if you wanted to."

"Could be but doing it this way's easier. Besides, you're needing a hand. You and Rex sure can't fight —"

"We can do the best we can — forting up inside this house, fighting them off until there's nothing left."

"Be plain foolish. Be you alone, you know that. Rex couldn't pull a trigger, shape he's in."

"I know, but if that's how it's to end, let it. You've already told us it was hopeless, that we couldn't beat Joe Keck, and I know you're right. But it doesn't change anything. To get our ranch he'll have to kill us both."

Rademacher swore softly. "You're both bull-headed as a mule — and you've sort've got me feeling the same way."

"Don't let us. No cause for you to throw your life away on something that means nothing to you."

"That's all got kind of swapped around inside my head, seems. Now, I want you to quit your worrying. Long as I'm on the place I'll look after things."

Abruptly Modesty looked away. "I — I don't want you to get hurt — die —"

"Not much in favor of it myself," he said, smiting, "but don't you go fretting about that. Can look out for myself, same as I aim to look out for you and Rex 'til you're over this hard spot. So it's settled. Thing to do now is get set."

She came back around to him quickly. "You think Keck will be back today?"

"Got my doubts. He'll figure we're expecting him to do just that, if he's the way you say he is. Like as not he'll hold off a spell, wait for tomorrow or even the next day, thinking to wind us up tight. That's good. Gives us time to get ready."

"How?"

"Was you that mentioned forting-up. Just what we'll do. Want you to get all the guns and bullets you've got, put them out here where they'll be handy."

Modesty nodded. "There are two or three rifles and a shotgun besides the pistols Rex and John carried now and then. I don't think we have many bullets, though."

That could be bad. He wasn't exactly long on cartridges himself, Rademacher realized, but he made no mention of it to the girl.

"Best we lay in a supply of water, too. Use tubs, buckets, pans — anything you can scare up. Keck's sure to try setting the house on fire and burning us out."

She paused, frowned. "But how could we get outside to fight the flames? They'll be waiting — shooting."

"Have to take our chances. Aim to pull that

spring wagon I saw down in the shed up in front of the door and turn it over. It'll give us some protection. I'll find something else for the back. . . . What was those chores that Rex claimed needed doing?"

"The herd has to be moved. He and John intended to do it several days ago."

"It real important?"

"I guess so. They were going to drive them up to a little valley north of here. Grass there hasn't been grazed on for over a year and they've pretty well worked over where they are."

"Where's that?"

"Southeast of here. The lower range we call it. Other things that have to be done are feeding and watering the yard stock — horses, pigs, the cow and the like. I can do that."

"Can see to it myself when I get back from moving the herd."

"It'll take you most of the day, and I need to do something, keep busy."

Tom nodded his understanding. "All right, long as you stick close to the house." He turned for the door, halted. "One thing more, we need a signal."

"Signal?"

"For just in case Keck outfigures us and shows up today. That happens, you get inside, close the doors and bar them. Then take one of the rifles and fire two quick shots out the back window. Understand?"

Modesty said, "The rifle, two shots."

"Yeh. Rifle sound carries farther and it has a different crack than a pistol. I hear it, I'll come fast. Best you keep your eyes open. Don't want Keck and his bunch slipping up on you."

"I will," the girl assured him. "You be careful, yourself."

"Sure," Rademacher said, smiling. It had been a long time since anyone had taken any interest in his welfare.

Chapter 9

Rademacher spent the next hour getting the wagon into position in front of the entrance to the house. For a bulwark at the rear, he brought up three large barrels that he found in the barn, lined them up side by side, and for lack of other available material, filled them with short logs from the woodpile.

Rock or soil would have offered greater protection but the use of such would have required considerable more time and he was anxious to get the cattle moved and return to the ranch before the day grew too old. If all remained peaceful, he might find the opportunity to add the more solid material to the wood in the hogsheads.

Astride the dun, he rode southeast as Modesty had directed, in search of the herd. The morning was still young and fresh and he took note again of the fine land and the condition of the grass and trees that grew upon it.

A great deal of wildflowers were in bloom — large clumps of white fleabane, purple verbena, bee-plant, pinwheel marigold and along the banks of a small creek draining into the river, were masses of crownbeard and sun-flowers. There was little evidence of snake-weed, always an indication of poor soil and overgrazing, except on an occasional rock ridge bursting out of the ground; and it was only there that he also noted cactus, both prickly pear and the taller, gaunt cholla. The Todds had prime property, that was certain, and while he had no idea of what Keck's Crosshatch range was like, it was easy to see why he coveted that owned by Rex and Modesty.

He fell to thinking of the girl as the dun loped steadily on. She had startled him doing that about-face and telling him pointblank that she did not want him to stay around. It had come as a surprise and for the first few moments he did not understand, then it had dawned on him that she was thinking of his personal safety.

That had shaken and in no small way disturbed Tom Rademacher. Somehow he had come to mean something more to her than a passing stranger, a fact that in itself he found difficult to comprehend; and while she stirred him as had no other woman he ever before had encountered, he knew he could not permit interest on the part of either of them to grow.

He had the matter of Gabe Claunch yet to

settle, the seeking out of his brother's murderer and squaring accounts with him for what he had done. That could take years, as it already had, and it would be unfair to Modesty to ask her to wait, stand by until he had completed his self-imposed task.

Too, there was no guarantee that once he had found Claunch he would come out of the confrontation alive. Claunch was no greenhorn; he was an experienced, hardened outlaw and the odds, when they came face to face, would likely be with him.

Should Pete Webber prove to be the man he sought the picture would, of course, change. Settlement would come quickly and either he would survive and the trail of vengeance he had pursued for so long would end — or he would be dead. He had little faith, however, in the possibility the two men were one and the same; luck was never that kind to him.

Chances were Webber was just another hardcase with a flair for handling a six-gun, and he would have no choice but to turn his back on Modesty, on the sort of life he hungered for, and ride on. Maybe, after he did finally overtake Claunch, and assuming he came out winner, he could return to the Sage River country and the Todds. If Modesty still felt as she did, perhaps they could pick up where matters had broken off — but that, too, had a catch; her being there hinged on his being able to prevent Joe Keck from driving the family off.

Tom's jaw tightened as he gave that thought. War with the rancher and his tough hired-hands was going to be no cinch deal. He would be on his own, with Rex down and unable to help, and he certainly didn't intend to let Modesty endanger herself. He'd have to go it alone, but he reckoned he could manage if the breaks didn't tip against him.

Forted up in the house with its thick, sturdy walls, given an ample number of guns placed strategically at the windows he could hold off a dozen men as long as ammunition held out. He recalled then what Modesty had said about their supply of bullets, and sobered. It would be a matter of making every shot count — which was the wrong way to do it if a man had any hope of turning back a large force of attackers; literally laying down a barrage of lead was the only sure way to discourage their efforts. Firing only occasionally and with care was a tip-off that ammunition was short.

But there was no answer other than to face the problem, do the best he could when Keck paid his return call, and so he pushed the worry aside. There was nothing to be gained by fretting over it.

A short time later he saw the cattle, small in total number as most herds go, but all sleek and fat and in excellent condition. The area was well grazed as Modesty had feared and the steers were already beginning to drift and forage farther out. Had they been neglected much longer there was no doubt the herd would have become badly scattered.

He had some difficulty getting the animals underway, accomplishing it by much shouting and the use of his rope, doubled to a short length and handled as a whip.

He had no idea of the exact spot the Todds intended to halt the herd on as he got it moving up a wide draw that angled off into a northwesterly direction but supposed any area where grass was plentiful would be satisfactory. It would be smart, he decided, to drive the cattle as near the house as possible; it would be easier to keep an eye on them should Joe Keck have any thoughts of running them off or sending in his men to shoot them.

The draw continued and the herd followed its course at a steady, plodding pace. Rademacher, off to one side out of the dust, kept his eyes ahead, searching for a likely spot to bring the drive to a halt. He wasn't too far from the house, he reckoned; it would lay just a mile or so beyond a rise to the east as near as he could figure. He could call a stop anytime now as the grass was good everywhere.

Abruptly Tom drew up as the silhouetted shape of a horse and rider on a hill to his left caught his attention. For a long minute he studied the man, and then leaving the cattle to shift for themselves, he cut back, circled well below the hill and came in on the trespasser from the opposite direction.

Hand resting on the butt of his pistol, he moved in closer at a quiet walk, gaze probing the rider as he sought to recognize him. He didn't appear to be one of those who had been with Joe Keck earlier that morning, but that he was a Crosshatch man was certain; the brand on the left hip of his horse proved that.

Digging spurs into the dun, Rademacher rushed forward suddenly, quickly covering the gap that separated him from the intruder. The rider, hearing the fast pound of his gelding's approach, twisted about hurriedly. His hand dropped to the pistol on his hip, fell slowly away as he saw Rademacher ready to draw.

"Now — wait a minute," he began nervously.

Tom smiled coldly. The puncher was young and definitely not one of those accompanying the rancher on either of the two visits to the Todds.

"You've got the notion, go ahead, try," he said.

The rider wagged his head. "No, sir, ain't about to. My ma raised no dumb kid."

"Seems she did else you wouldn't be here trespassing on other folks' land. Could get you killed quick the way things are around here right now."

"Sort of figured that when the foreman told me to come over here. Sure weren't no idea of mine."

"Was Keck's I reckon. Why'd he send you?"

"Ain't knowing for certain. Just told me to lope over here and have a look-see at the Todds' herd then let him know how big it was and where it was grazing."

"That all?"

"Yes, sir, that's it!"

Tom nodded. The rancher apparently did have ideas about the Todd cattle. It would be smart to leave them where they were, perhaps drift them even nearer to the ranchhouse.

"Expect you knew you'd be trespassing and could earn yourself a bullet —"

"Truth is, mister, I didn't do no thinking on it. I only done what I was told. That's all I'm paid for." The puncher shrugged, looked off across the rolling land. "Nobody told me things was this touchy."

"They're worse, and I ought to put a slug in both your legs and send you back to Keck as a warning, but I'm feeling big-hearted today. You turn around and light out for Crosshatch and when you see that foreman or Joe Keck, you say you never found the Todd's herd and you don't know where it is."

"But he —"

"You do that and you can keep on living and walking. Don't, and I'll look you up later on. That plain?"

"Sure is, mister. It all right if I pull out right now?"

"Probably be the smart thing to do. I might get to thinking over this big-heartedness of mine and change my mind."

The puncher swallowed hard, bobbed his head, and wheeling about, struck off northward at a fast lope. Tom watched him until he disappeared beyond a roll of land and then doubled back to where he had left the cattle. Sending the young rider back with the instructions he'd given him would not stop whatever plans Keck had for the Todds' herd, he knew; he'd simply dispatch another man on the same mission.

And if the puncher reported what he had seen and told that he'd been turned back, it would work out just as well. Keck would get the idea the cattle were being watched over and that could change his thinking about staging a raid.

He was well satisfied with where he was leaving the herd. They were feeding in a broad, shallow swale on a slope that slanted gently toward the east. As the animals grazed they would work even nearer to the ranch-house; it would be easy to make occasional rides to the low ridge west of the buildings and have a look at them.

Taking a final swing around the area to see if there were any more Crosshatch hired-hands prowling about and finding none, he turned in the direction of the ranch. He'd not tell Modesty about Keck's man, nor would he explain why he had brought the herd in close instead of driving it farther north as she'd directed. Such would only worry her and she had more than enough on her mind as it was.

Chapter 10

Modesty had finished the job of filling containers with water and was assembling the family stock of weapons and ammunition when Rademacher returned. Pausing in the doorway he glanced about the room giving her preparations his approval.

"You're back early," she said, frowning. "Was there something wrong? Is the herd —"

"Everything's fine," he replied quickly. "Maybe I didn't push your cows as far north as you wanted but they're in a good spot. Things all right here?"

"If you mean Keck there's been no sign of him."

"How's Rex?"

The girl sighed heavily. "I don't think he's any better. Getting up like he did — and then falling, tore the wounds open. . . . Are you hungry?"

Rademacher brushed at the sweat on his face, shook his head. "Don't usually feed myself in the middle of the day. Used to breakfasting and then eating supper. I can hold out 'til then. Looks like you've got things all set."

"Almost. . . . I wish we had more bullets."

"We'll manage. Could be we're doing all this for nothing. Might not come down to shooting."

He said it only in the hopes of cheering her. In his mind he knew Keck would not back off now; the man could not afford to.

Returning to the yard Tom spent another hour or so strengthening the fortifications in the back of the house by adding more logs and the few rocks that were available to the line of barrels. Giving the matter further thought, he scattered a few piles of wood at various, nearby points for use should it become necessary to reach the sides of the structure.

That done to his satisfaction, and noting the lateness of the day, he fed the stock, relieving Modesty of the chore and then, returning to his quarters, took stock of his own supply of ammunition. He found he had a half box of cartridges for the rifle, somewhat less for the pistol he wore.

He could be in better shape, he thought as he placed the long gun with its spare shells on a table pulled up close to the doorway. If it wasn't so risky he'd make a fast ride to Coyote Crossing that night and buy up a fresh supply, but such meant leaving Modesty and Rex alone for several hours and that didn't appeal to him.

Filling all of the loops in his belt, he took what pistol shells were left, tied them in a spare bandana and shoved them into a side pocket of his pants, and then stepped out into the yard. Darkness was not far off and as he stood there in the quiet staring off into the shadowy distance, listening to the hushed sounds of the coming night, Modesty called him to supper.

She was strangely silent during the meal and he guessed her mind was occupied with thoughts of what the coming day might bring. He tried to reassure her as best he could but had little success and after a decent interval, excused himself, knowing she was tired and claiming the same for himself.

He went first to the cabin as if intending to seek out his bed, settled instead in a chair near the window from which he had a good view of the house. When the lights all finally winked out, he arose, and going to the barn, mounted the still saddled dun gelding. Walking him quietly across the hardpack, he cut a course due west for a last look at the herd. He still didn't think Keck would make a move that soon but when you dealt with a man such as him, Tom thought it best to take nothing for granted.

The cattle had bedded down in the deepest

part of the swale where he had left them. Circling farther, he gained the highest point of the ridge behind them where he would have an unobstructed view of the herd and dismounted. There, hunched on his heels, he set up a watch.

It was pleasantly warm. The sky was clear of clouds and littered with stars that, aided by a half moon, spread a pale, silver glow over the land. Coyotes barked in the hills to the west and now and then a night bird called plaintively into the quiet. It all put him at ease, despite the tenseness of the situation, and filled him with a contentedness he had long ago forgotten while a dull, lonely ache once made itself known within him.

This was what he had once planned to make of his life — a ranch of his own, a herd of cattle, and a family after he had gotten the herd, beginning time out of the way. But it had all been washed aside and lost in the blast of a six-gun. . . . Would he ever again get the chance to realize that dream?

It was there now, waiting, his for the taking. Tom Rademacher knew that, not in the vein of conceit, but in a practical realization of what Modesty Todd had come to mean to him, and he to her. Yet inside him was a hard stubbornness, an unbending determination that stolidly refused to concede. Always when such moments were upon him and a reason for forsaking the search filled his mind, the remembrance of Virgil and his death and Gabe Claunch who had brought it about, pushed to the fore, soon crowding out all else.

And somewhere deep in his heart a voice would make itself heard, telling him he could not abandon the purpose he had undertaken, that conscience would give him no rest should he ever try. It was a sacred obligation and there could be no shirking it, but the dream always died hard and each succeeding time it was more difficult to ignore. Such was doubly true in that instance; heretofore there had been no woman involved — now there was Modesty Todd.

Rising finally, Rademacher mounted his horse and made a circuit of the sleeping cattle. His gaze was not on them however, but scanned the surrounding country for signs of riders. He saw no one, and eventually pulling away, loped the gelding toward a higher rise to the north.

Long before he reached the desired point the red eye of a campfire glowing in the distance drew his sharp concern. It was well to the west, along a line of bluffs. He gave it thoughtful consideration, concluded after a time that it would not be any of Joe Keck's hands; they would not be building any fires.

Likely it was only some passing pilgrim, much like himself, camping for the night.

Continuing on to the knoll he once more halted, had his painstaking search of the silent, silvered land, and satisfied there was no one else in the area, headed back to the ranch. Was there not the possibility of Keck striking first at the house, he would have stayed near the cattle since there was no doubt now the rancher had entertained thoughts of putting on a raid. He would have to risk the possibility however; Modesty and Rex came first.

Entering the yard he stabled the dun, and suddenly aware of weariness, sought out his bed. He had scarcely closed his eyes it seemed when a hand shaking his shoulder brought him upright. It was Modesty.

Chapter 11

"What's wrong?"

The girl drew back, features taut and strained, eyes bright with worry. "It's Rex — he's worse. He woke me up tossing and turning. I went in to see about him and he's out of his head and burning with fever."

"That settles it," Rademacher declared decisively. "I'm going after that doctor."

Modesty turned for the doorway. "Hurry, Tom," she called over her shoulder. "Please hurry."

Rademacher dressed quickly. The doctor would have to come to the ranch; Rex was now in too poor a condition to be moved. He should have insisted on getting medical aid that first day, he told himself bitterly — or, better yet, he could have loaded both Modesty and her brother into the wagon and driven them into town. But it was too late to think about that now — and likely the girl wouldn't have been willing to leave, anyway. She would have wanted to stay on the ranch.

Grim, not liking the thought of leaving her alone now with a helpless brother on her hands for several hours, he strapped on his gun and trotted to the house. He found the girl in the bedroom applying wet cloths to Todd's forehead. The man was raving incoherently and his skin had a bright, scarlet look. Modesty glanced up worriedly as Tom entered.

"I don't know what else to do for him," she said in a ragged voice.

"Expect that's the best thing. I'll head out now, get Ross, or whatever his name is."

"That's him. You'll find his house near the end of the street. Has his office in the front."

Rademacher turned to go, paused, frowning. "Don't like leaving you here. Be about my luck Keck and his bunch will come soon as I'm out of sight."

"There's nothing else we can do," Modesty said. "I'll bar the doors and windows."

"Just what I want you to do, and if he does show up, try to stall him, keep him talking so's I'll have time to get back. Aim to pick up some bullets while I'm in town. Anything else you're needing?"

Modesty got slowly to her feet. "Well, yes, there is. We're low on groceries — out of some things, in fact. John planned to go after them the other day and then the trouble started."

"Expect I ought to get what you need.

Could find ourselves forted up in here for a spell."

"You'll have to take the buckboard —"

Rademacher swore silently. He had intended to cut across country, ignore the road in the interest of saving time. Even in a light wagon he would have to stick to the regular route.

"Too much to carry on a saddle?"

"I'm afraid so. If you think it best we could let the supplies go until later."

"Don't think that'd be smart. Be natural for Keck to try starving us out when he sees he's getting nowheres with guns. Got a list of what you need?"

Modesty hurried into the kitchen, took a folded sheet of paper off one of the shelves and handed it to him. "Here's the one I made out for John. Mr. Kiefer, he's the store owner, will have to add it onto our bill. We haven't settled up with him now for some time, but I don't think he'll mind. Just as soon as Rex is on his feet we'll sell off some steers and pay him."

Rademacher said, "I'll tell him," and looked closely at the girl. "Sure don't like doing this at all but I guess we've got no choice. Soon as I'm gone you close this house tight — and stay inside no matter what."

"I will — and, Tom, you be careful, too."

He nodded, said, "Be back soon as I can," and stepped out into the yard.

"Take the gray, the mare," Modesty called after him. "She's used to pulling the buckboard."

Tom entered the barn, located the horse indicated and hurriedly threw the harness into place. Then leading the wiry little mount to the shed, hitched her to the light vehicle. Shortly he was pulling out of the yard and striking for the road. As he whirled off he glanced back. Modesty was standing on the stoop, partly obscured by the wagon he had overturned in front of the house. She waved, and after he had given his salute, stepped back inside and closed the door.

He hadn't thought to ask Modesty for specific directions, he thought as the mare sped along at a good trot. In his haste to get on the way and return it had not occurred to him, but, logically, there would be only one road leading into town and he unquestioningly was on it.

The low, rolling range land was beginning to break up and become more hilly with deeper draws and steep faced buttes. There was no sign of other ranches or even of cattle and he guessed he was in that part of the Sage River Valley that was unused and unclaimed by anyone.

The gray slowed as the road began to climb toward a distant crest. Brush hemmed in the wheel tracks on both sides and the ground itself became progressively rougher while scattered boulders littered the slopes. The loss of speed irritated him and he began to urge the mare on. But by now he couldn't be too far from Coyote Crossing, he assured himself, and there was no sense in killing the little mare.

He eased up, let the horse settle into her own slow but steady pace. The summit was less than a mile ahead and he should be able to regain some of the lost time on the downgrade. Half turning, Rademacher looked back, wondering at the length of the climb. He stiffened.

Three riders were in sight at the foot of the long slope. It could mean nothing — only pilgrims or local cowpunchers on their way to town also; and it might mean much — Crosshatch riders keeping an eye on him.

Taut, a deep fear for the safety of Modesty beginning to gnaw at his insides, he studied the men, striving to make out their identities. They were too far off; he could tell nothing of them or the horses they rode.

Coming back around, he looked beyond the bobbing head of the mare. The top of the hill was only yards away. Brushing at the sweat on his face, he weighed the advisability of pulling off into the brush, allowing the men to draw abreast where he could determine who they were. He shook his head; it would accomplish little — and he would lose precious time.

That they were not trying to stop him was evident since they were not pressing their horses but merely keeping pace with the buckboard. Like as not they were no more than travelers on the same road, bent for town as was he.

He settled back on the seat of the light vehicle as the mare gained the summit and started the roll downward. He'd waste no time on them, whoever they were, but somehow he couldn't dismiss them entirely from his mind. Where had they come from? That question troubled him most of all. He had seen no one as he passed along the road, yet they were suddenly there. Had they been hiding, waiting for him to pass, after which they swung in behind?

If so, for what reason? That they did not intend to stop him from reaching Coyote Crossing was evident; the small scatter of structures that was the settlement was now in sight and less than a mile distant. What then would be their reason for trailing him?

Rademacher shrugged. He reckoned he was

edgy, turned so by his concern for Modesty. Best thing to do was forget the riders, whoever they were, attend to business and get back to the Todd ranch as quickly as possible.

He swung into the end of the town's single, main street, eyes switching back and forth to the few houses that lined its sides. A sign, A. ROSS, M.D., caught his attention and he wheeled up to the hitchrack immediately. Taking a turn around the whipstock with the reins, he jumped down, hurried to the dust-clogged screen door that faced the street.

Pulling it open, Tom stepped inside. A graying pleasant looking woman rose from a chair in what was apparently the patient's waiting room to greet him.

"The doc — he here?"

The woman smiled, laid aside the knitting she was working at. "No, I'm sorry, He's not here at the moment. I'm Mrs. Ross. Can I help —"

"I'm from the Todd ranch. Rex needs him bad."

The doctor's wife frowned. "What's the trouble?"

"Gunshot. He's in a bad way this morning."

"That's too bad. When did it happen?"

"Couple of days ago. Can you tell me where I'll find the doc?"

"He went to deliver a baby. Mrs. Carver's.

They live north of town."

"I've got to find him — get him here fast!" Rademacher stopped, seeing no point in wasting more time with the physician's wife. "How do I find the Carvers'?"

Mrs. Ross shook her head. "I'll send our hired man after him. It will save time. You go on back — and tell Modesty not to worry."

That was a better idea. "Fine," Tom said. "Got to pick up some stuff at the general store. Maybe he'll be here by the time I'm ready to pull out."

"Likely he won't come this way. He'll save an hour or more by cutting across the hills. Chances are he'll get there before you do."

Tension gripping Rademacher eased slightly. He smiled, touched the brim of his hat. "Obliged to you, ma'am. Takes a big load off my mind. Rex is in a bad way and I'll appreciate it if you'll send word to the doc to hurry."

"I'll do that. . . . Are Modesty and John all right?"

Tom paused as he turned away. "She's fine — worried. John's dead."

Mrs. Ross started visibly. "Dead! What —"

"Joe Keck and his crowd. There was a shooting. John wasn't as lucky as Rex."

"Oh, my God!" the woman moaned in a low voice. "I just supposed it was an accident of some kind — but it was those men, those terrible men! Please tell Modesty that I'm sorry, that I'll drive out soon as I can."

"She'd like that," Tom said, moving on, "but I reckon you'd best wait a few days. Trouble's not over yet."

Pushing open the screen, he descended the sagging wood steps to the yard and crossed to where the mare and buckboard waited. As he climbed up and onto the seat and reached for the leathers, his eyes narrowed.

Three riders were pulling up to the rack fronting the Silver Saddle Saloon. Two were familiar — Sackett and Hatton. Both had been with Joe Keck at the Todd place the morning of the shooting. The third man was a stranger to him but undoubtedly was also one of the rancher's hired guns since he was riding a horse bearing the Crosshatch brand.

These were the three he'd seen pull in behind him on the hill and again a question rose in his mind; was it only by accident or had they done so intentionally?

Chapter 12

Rademacher watched the trio dismount and wind their reins around the crossbar. Then, stepping lazily up onto the saloon's porch, they crossed and shouldered their way through the swinging doors. It was all done with a painstaking indifference and none had bothered to glance in his direction — the realization of which immediately stirred a warning within Tom.

There was something on the wind. Joe Keck had sent the riders to keep watch over him. His eyes narrowed as a cool sort of anger filled him. Likely they had other instructions, too; he'd see what he could do about it just as soon as he handed Modesty's list over to Kiefer.

Pulling away from the doctor's, Tom drove the short distance down the street to the general store and again drew to a halt. As he crossed to the door he threw a glance at the Silver Saddle. Sackett, Hatton and the third Crosshatch rider were standing just inside the saloon's entrance. All were now watching him.

Jaw set, Rademacher stepped into the merchandise littered store. Kiefer, a small, balding man wearing a denim bib apron to protect his clothing, looked up from a counter at the rear of the room.

"Something I can do for you?"

Tom dug Modesty's list out of his shirt pocket and passed it to the merchant. "I'm from the Todds'. Be obliged if you'll fill this order right away. I'm in sort of a hurry."

Kiefer frowned as he studied the list. "Quite a bit here," he said, hesitantly. "Afraid I can't —"

Rademacher waited, considering the man coldly. "You can't what?" he prompted quietly.

The merchant folded the sheet of paper, laid it on the counter. "Can't accommodate the Todds. Bill is getting big and they ain't paid up in more'n seven months."

"They always do, don't they?"

"Well, yes, but the account is getting out of hand."

"Expect you'll get your money sure enough. Modesty said they'd pay up soon as Rex could sell off a few steers. He's laid up."

"So I heard."

Tom looked closely at the man. "You hear about it — that John had been shot dead and

Rex was down with a couple of bullet holes in him?"

Kiefer shifted nervously on his feet. "Heard some of the Crosshatch boys talking —"

"You for certain it wasn't Joe Keck himself telling you, and telling you, too, not to give the Todds any more credit?"

The storekeeper's face flushed. "This here's my place and I run it the way —"

"You do just what Keck tells you," Rademacher cut in disgustedly and moved back to the front of the building. Glancing up and down the street he saw that Kiefer's was the sole supply house in evidence; it was either buy from him or travel to the next town, and there was no time to spare for that.

"How about me? He tell you not to sell to me, too?"

Kiefer shrugged. "Seeing as how you're a stranger I don't figure —"

"All right then, take care of the order. Have it ready for me in fifteen minutes — and add a box of forty-fours and another'n of forty-five cartridges to it."

The storekeeper did not stir. Tom gave him a hard grin. "It'll be cash."

Kiefer bobbed his head, took up the list. "It'll be waiting for you," he said and began to select the items ordered from his shelves.

Rademacher wheeled, doubled back to the

door. Stepping out onto the porch, he moved off it and pointed for the saloon, stride long and purposeful and drawing some measure of attention from the few persons along the board sidewalks.

Reaching the Silver Saddle he mounted the landing, noting as he did that Keck's men were no longer visible above the batwings, and pushed through.

Except for the three riders and a bartender the place was deserted. Tom, pausing briefly to let his eyes adjust, gave them all a quick, calculating glance and crossed to the counter. . . . He'd been right; the redhead was Sackett, the lean, balding one with the colorless look was Hatton. The remaining Crosshatch hand was still a stranger and had not been in either of the parties that had ridden into Todds'.

Bellying up to the bar Tom made a motion to the aproned man behind it. "Whiskey — the good kind, not any of your rotgut."

The saloonkeeper registered no reaction, reached for a bottle and poured a shot-glass brimful. Sliding it slowly into place before Tom, he said, "Two-bits."

Rademacher reached into a pocket for a coin, glanced on the Crosshatch riders at the opposite end of the counter. "Take out for another'n," he said.

Tossing off the first portion, he held the

thick bottomed container between thumb and forefinger while the bartender refilled it. Tipping it to his lips he downed the liquor in a single gulp, set the glass on the counter. Picking up his change, he dropped it into his shirt pocket and sauntered casually along the bar to where the Crosshatch riders stood.

"Best you be enjoying your drinking," he drawled, pulling out into the room where he could face them.

The men pivoted slowly, warily. Hatton, chin thrust forward said, "What's that mean?"

"Means it's going to be your last if I catch you dogging my tracks again."

Hatton shot a glance at his companions. "Who says we was?"

"Me — and I'm a long way from being blind. Don't know what Keck told you to do but if you want to keep on living stay out of my sight from now on."

Hatton bristled. "Now, hold on a mite there, mister! There ain't nobody tells me —"

"I am," Rademacher said coldly.

Sackett pushed his hat to the back of his head, doing so with deliberate care. "I ain't so good at taking advice either. Neither is Hank. You figure you can make us all three swallow it?"

"No sweat."

Hatton swore softly. "By God, you sure got a big opinion of yourself! Just because you got the jump on us at the Todds' when we wasn't looking sure don't mean you can do it starting even."

"Could be and right now'd be a good time to find out. Fact is, thinking on it, I'm willing to give you the start — all of you. Sure don't want no advantage."

The balding Hatton frowned. He looked at Sackett and then at the one the redhead had called Hank uncertainly.

"You saying you'll take on all three of us at the same time?"

Tom nodded. "And let you have the jump," he replied, and stepping back a few more paces, allowed his hands to drop to his sides. "Your move."

In the dead silence that followed the Crosshatch men hung motionless. Somewhere down the street an anvil rang methodically as a blacksmith plied his trade.

Abruptly Hank shook his head. "Don't go counting me in on no shootout. I ain't asking for trouble."

"You've got it anyway," Rademacher snapped. "Riding for Joe Keck saddles you with it, but if you want out then draw your iron, real easy like and lay it up there on the bar."

Hank complied, handling his weapon gingerly as if it was hot metal. Tom kept his steady gaze on Hatton and the redhead.

"Sort of makes the odds even better for me. You about ready?"

Sackett swore deeply, and his hands raised and in full view, wheeled about and placed his back to Rademacher. Hatton continued to stare for a long half minute, and then, lifting his arms, also turned away.

Tom took a deep breath. It had been a tight few moments and he'd thought once they were going to call his hand.

"Fair enough," he said quietly. "Now keep on being smart and stay off my trail. Next time I won't be giving you your choosings."

Coming about on a heel, he moved for the swinging doors while tension again rose within him. His back offered a good target, an easy one, but he knew he could not look around, show the slightest concern. If he did the impression he had built would vanish instantly.

He reached the entrance, paused briefly, and then elbowed through the batwings onto the porch. Only then did he turn back his glance. Keck's men had not stirred.

Chapter 13

Kiefer was waiting for him in the front of his store when Rademacher returned. Nearby were several boxes containing Modesty's order and the cartridges which Tom had specified.

"It all there?" he asked, reaching for his money.

The storekeeper nodded. "Everything that was on the list. Be twelve dollars, including the shells."

Tom dug deeper, produced a double-eagle. Kiefer made change from a sack he carried in a pocket, bobbed. "Obliged. . . . That your buckboard out front?"

Rademacher made no reply, his attention now on Sackett, Hatton and the rider called Hank. They had mounted their horses, were passing slowly down the street. He watched them go by — heading back out the way they had come.

"Be glad to give you a hand."

Tom swung his glance back to Kiefer, nodded, and taking up as many boxes as he could manage, and followed by the merchant with the remainder, returned to the buck-board. Storing the cartons well forward in the bed, he nodded absently to Kiefer's repeated thanks and climbed onto the seat. Keck's men would be ahead of him on the return trip, he realized as he unwound the reins, and he had no liking for that.

That, too, could mean nothing. He could be wrong about the rancher putting them on his trail; they could have been telling the truth and simply ridden into town for a drink. They had made no attempt to interfere with his actions, but that failure could be explained by his taking the play away from them in the saloon. Shrugging in exasperation, Rade-macher wheeled the buckboard about; it was always the uncertainties, the not knowing for sure that got to a man.

Clucking the mare into a trot, he moved hurriedly down the dusty lane that lay between Coyote Crossing's weathered buildings. A few persons paused to stare at his passage, recognizing him for a stranger and wondering at his presence, no doubt. As he rolled past the jail he noted the figure leaning in the doorway — a young, slouching man who looked more like a fence rider than a lawman. More than likely he had been one of Joe Keck's cowhands before the deputy's star was pinned on him.

Reaching the end of the street, Rademacher cut the buckboard onto the road west and began the long climb to the crest of the ridge separating the flat where the town lay from the Sage River Valley.

Hatton and his two friends were already out of sight and that bit of knowledge brought a quick frown to Tom's sun and wind burned features. They had not had time enough to reach the summit and drop over onto the yonder slope; it could only mean they had turned off, were somewhere in the brush and rocks that covered the land.

The mare slowed, settled into a steady, fast walk up the grade. Rademacher, eyes continually whipping back and forth over the rugged country, hitched the forty-five on his hip forward to a more readily accessible position, the conviction that he could expect trouble growing stronger with each passing moment.

Turning his head he glanced up at the sky. It was near mid-day. He had already been gone from the ranch several hours and more would elapse before he could complete the return trip. Such gave Keck ample time to do whatever it was he planned, if, indeed, that was what this was all about.

He took some comfort, however, in the knowledge that he had left Modesty well prepared for a raid. She had only to keep the doors and windows locked and thereby placed herself in a position to hold out indefinitely — assuming the rancher didn't resort to fire. Such was entirely possible, Tom realized grimly. That the girl was alone with a helpless, injured man would mean nothing to Keck.

He glanced back. Half the grade had been covered and there was still no sign of the three men. Again he gave consideration to the thought that he could be wrong, that Keck's riders had simply cut off across country and were in no way interested in him.

It was possible, but he found he couldn't accept the idea. Joe Keck would leave nothing undone to make possible his taking over the Todd ranch, and he had presented himself as an obstacle to that end. It was only logical to believe the rancher would want him out of the way.

Three quarters of the distance behind him. . . . Not too far to the summit. If the Crosshatch riders were somewhere on the slope they would be forced to show themselves soon as the rough, ragged terrain afforded only one crossing to the opposite side. It would be necessary for them to draw in, use the trail, and when they did that he would be able to see them.

He would, assuming they were still there

and had not, as he had considered earlier, swung off across country.

That faint hope died in the next breath. He straightened to attention as a rider appeared just below the crest, breaking out of the brush and rocks. Squinting against the glare, Tom recognized Sackett. Even as he watched two more horsemen rode into view — Hank and Enos Hatton. All were moving at a leisurely pace.

Rademacher studied them intently. Sackett, reaching the topmost point of the grade first, halted, evidently waiting for the others to catch up. He could see the Crosshatch rider looking back down the slope, eyes undoubtedly upon the slowly climbing mare and buckboard.

The three came together. For several moments they remained in the cut, silhouetted against the clean, blue sky beyond, and then suddenly all were gone.

Rademacher cursed impatiently, wishing he were nearer the summit and in a position to see what the men did next. Taking up the whip he urged the little horse to a faster gait. It made little difference. They were on the steepest part of the climb and the mare could do no better.

It seemed to take an hour but eventually they reached the crest, and with the gray heaving and flecked with sweat, Tom drew the buckboard to a stop. Rising to full height, he looked down the lengthy, winding road that unrolled below him. There was no one to be seen.

Muttering, he settled back on the seat to breathe the mare. His suspicions were again running strong. If Hatton and the others planned an ambush they had chosen an ideal location for it. Tall brush and large boulders flanked the road, extended far back from its shoulders offering dense and perfect cover for anyone not wishing to be seen.

There was only one thing in his favor; he would be moving downgrade and the gray could run fast and free with the buckboard. He guessed the Crosshatch men had thought of that, too, had weighed the disadvantage against laying their trap on the steep side of the ridge and ruled it out. It added up about even, he supposed, but for himself he preferred it this way; it was far better being forced into a wild dash downhill than being caught with a tired horse on a steep climb.

The mare had recovered her wind. Tom put her into motion and they rolled forward over the narrow strip of near level ground and dropped off onto the slope. Again Rademacher began a diligent search of the country adjacent to the road, probing for the slightest bit of movement, of color — anything that would betray the location of the ambush.

If there was an ambush. . . . Rademacher stirred in exasperation, once more angered by the uncertainty of it all. Everything was *if!* Why the hell couldn't it be clear-cut, out in the open so he wouldn't be filled with wonder and whether —

The sharp, close-by crack of a pistol shattered his thoughts. Wood splintered off the edge of the buckboard's seat as a bullet smashed against it, sang off into space.

Tom snatched his weapon from its holster, swept the surrounding land for a glimpse of the marksman. He saw no one, and rising to a crouch, slapped the mare's rump smartly with the reins, breaking her into a dead run.

More gunshots racketed across the slope. Rademacher felt the breath of a bullet against his forearm, heard the dull thunk of others driving into the buckboard's bed. The shots were coming from a mound of rock and brush to his right, he thought, but he could see no one and was thus unsure.

The firing continued. He hung there in the wildly swaying vehicle, reins gripped in one hand, pistol in the other, helpless against an unseen enemy who was targeting him relentlessly. A slug clipped through the brim of his hat, another tore at his sleeve.

He was done for unless he could get out of sight or range. He looked ahead to a slight bend in the road. Off its edge he could see a small flat on the shoulder where previous travelers had halted to rest their tired horses. . . . If he could make that, throw himself into the nearby brush. . . .

Hunched low, he urged the mare to a faster speed. The curve raced to meet him, and hauling him back hard on the leathers, he swung the buckboard onto the shoulder. The light vehicle bounced, sloughed dangerously to one side. The right rear wheel struck against a rock, cracked ominously. In the next instant Tom Rademacher felt himself soaring through space as the buckboard overturned.

Chapter 14

Rademacher crashed head-on into a clump of rabbit-bush. The tough, springy shrub gave under his weight, breaking his fall. Breath gone but unhurt, he rolled clear. A few paces away the buckboard was on its side, two wheels spinning slowly, its contents strewn nearby. The mare, miraculously, was still standing, the vehicle's shafts and harness twisted about her.

Somewhere across the road Tom heard a shout. He lunged to his feet, and pistol in hand, darted into the dense growth on his right.

"You sure you got him?"

It was Hatton's voice. A moment later Tom heard Sackett's peevish reply.

"Hell, yes, I'm sure! You seen the way that buckboard took off the road, didn't you?"

They were drawing nearer, moving slowly, not too certain of their safety despite the red-headed Sackett's confidence that one of his bullets had scored.

Where was Hank?

Rademacher, hunched in the brush, peered

through the sage green foliage endeavoring to locate the third Crosshatch rider. Hatton and Sackett were off to his left as near as he could tell but there was no sign of their partner — and before he could make a move toward them he must know his whereabouts.

"Well, we ain't never going to know nothing just setting here," Hatton said. "You circle around through them cedars. I'll work in from this side."

"What about Hank?"

"He'll be showing up pretty quick. Sent him on ahead to wait, just in the case that jasper got by us. Joe said he didn't want him coming back to the Todds no matter what it took."

Fear gripped Rademacher. It had all been planned, as he had suspected. Evidently Keck and his riders had been somewhere close-by when he drove off for town in the buckboard. By sheer accident he had played right into the rancher's hands.

Hatton, Sackett and Hank had then been sent to prevent his return while the remaining party went ahead with whatever it was that Joe Keck had in mind for the Todds.

"Ain't no use of him waiting," Sackett declared. "That bird won't be going nowheres."

"Maybe. Best we see for sure," Hatton answered.

Tom, grim with worry over Modesty and

Rex, drew himself up slowly. The men were moving toward the clearing on the shoulder. He could hear the dull thud of their horses' hooves on the baked ground. Sackett would be coming directly at him, circling as Hatton had directed. Taut, he waited. . . . He needed to get both of Keck's men off his back and be on his way to the Todds as soon as possible. That Modesty needed him was certain now.

The dry slap of brush brought Rademacher around swiftly. Almost immediately a horse broke into view in the underbrush, head bobbing up and down as it picked its way through the growth. A moment later Sackett, leaning forward, eyes fixed in the direction of the clearing, came into sight.

Tom withheld his fire. Knocking the man off his saddle with a bullet would be easy but the report would warn Hatton, send him rushing off into the brush and creating more delay — and he still had Hank, waiting somewhere down the road, to reckon with.

Frozen, Rademacher allowed the rider to move by. Muscles taut, he held off until Sackett's shoulders were to him and then, holding his pistol as a club, he slipped in behind the man's horse. He caught up quickly. The sound of his movements, however slight, brought the Crosshatch rider around. Surprise blanked his face as he saw Tom reaching for him. A startled yell broke from his lips as he was dragged from the saddle. It died abruptly as Rademacher's weapon slammed into the side of his head.

"Sam — that you?"

Kneeling beside the senseless man, Tom rode out the moments. Hatton had heard the yell. He could come to investigate but he could choose to ignore it, assuming it to be no more than an angry curse brought to his partner's lips by tripped brush whipping against him or for some other cause. It made little difference which he elected to follow.

"Sam! There was something wrong? Goddammit — answer me!"

Hatton's aggravated voice came from the fringe of tangled growth only a few feet away. He was moving in to see what, if anything, was wrong. Rademacher rose silently, stepped into the open.

"Hatton," he called softly.

The gunman whirled. His hand came up fast, metal glinting off the pistol he held.

Tom fired once. The empty eyed rider rocked on his saddle. Reflex action of his muscles triggered the weapon he clutched, sent a bullet driving into the ground beside him. His horse shied wildly, setting him to swaying precariously. Abruptly Hatton buckled, toppled, fell heavily into the brush as his mount trotted off toward that of Sackett's.

Rademacher wheeled, hurried back to the clearing. The mare, trapped by the upset buckboard, had not moved. Putting his shoulder to the vehicle, he righted it, and, aware that there could still be need for the supplies he'd purchased, spent the next few precious moments collecting the items and tossing them into the light wagon's bed. That done, he climbed back onto the seat and returned to the road.

Only then did he recall the crackling sound he'd heard when a wheel had struck a rock, but it was too late to do anything about it. He would have to chance a breakdown, and if such occurred, he'd strip the harness from the mare and ride her bareback to the ranch.

Hank. . . .

The man was somewhere further down the grade, according to what he'd overheard Hatton say — and there was no way of avoiding him. Drawing his pistol again, Tom crouched low on the seat as the mare galloped along the steep road. The Crosshatch rider could be anywhere, hiding among the rocks, waiting in the thick brush, holding off until he could get the clean, open shot that he wanted. It was like being a clay rabbit in a shooting gallery, Rademacher thought wryly.

111

Halfway down from the crest. . . . Tom frowned, puzzled. He had expected to hear from Hank before reaching that point. The brush and rocks on the slope were beginning to thin out and shortly there would be fewer places in which an ambush could be laid.

As if in answer to his wonder, a gunshot flatted hollowly above the drumming of the mare's hooves and the slicing grind of the buckboard's iron-tired wheels. Tom felt a searing pain across his arm, threw himself off the seat.

Directly ahead a rider spurted into view, coming from behind the last large mound of rocks. It was Hank. Seeing Rademacher lunge forward and now half on and half off the seat, he evidently thought his bullet had found its mark.

As the vehicle swept nearer, Rademacher rose suddenly. Hank drew back sharply in surprise, whipped up his pistol. Tom, bracing himself as best he could in the bouncing, rocking buckboard, steadied his forty-five on a crooked arm and triggered a shot. Hank jolted as the bullet smashed into him. His weapon fell from his hand, and hauling back on the reins of his horse, he whirled about and disappeared behind the formation.

Still low, Tom kept his gun ready as the galloping mare drew abreast the mound. Hank had been hit but it appeared to be no serious wound, and while he had lost his pistol, he undoubtedly still had a rifle in the boot of his saddle.

There was no sign of the man. He was not behind the pile of rocks or anywhere near it. He must have retreated hurriedly into the brush farther on.

Rademacher sighed in relief, pulled himself back onto the seat. He'd made it past Keck's bushwhackers, and likely he'd encounter no more of the rancher's hired-hands during the remainder of the trip. But he'd take no chances on it, he decided, punching out the empties in his gun and thumbing fresh cartridges into the cylinder. He'd be ready if more trouble was to come.

The gray reached the bottom of the grade still at a fast gait. She slowed as Tom drew her in gently. There was no profit in letting her run herself into the ground, and he was not forgetting that weakened wheel. Twisting about, he glanced at it; it appeared to be solid enough even though slightly crooked.

An hour later he topped out the last rise barring the valley proper and began the final leg of the journey. A black smudge in the sky, noticed only casually earlier, was now becoming more pronounced. He studied it, striving to figure the location of its source. It had seemed too far east for the Todd place, but now from a different angle, he was not so sure.

And then, as more miles slipped beneath the pounding hooves of the mare and he reached the last flat leading up to the ranch, it became certain. The Todd place had been put to the torch.

Chapter 15

The house with all its contents had been burned to the ground, was now only smouldering embers from which black trailers of smoke twisted up into the sky. Fear gripped Rademacher. What of Modesty and Rex? Had they been trapped inside the structure? Lashing the mare to top speed, he raced up the road, anxious to reach the ruin but dreading what he might find.

He reached the yard, wheeled into it, caught sight of two figures, one prone, the other bending over it. The clawing concern within him eased. It was Modesty and Rex. The man lay on a pallet with the girl crouched beside him. At least they had not been caught in the flames. Bringing the gray to a halt, he leaped from the buckboard and raced toward them.

"Are you hurt?" he shouted as he drew near.

Modesty turned stunned features to him. For a long moment she simply stared, and then abruptly the dam burst. Tears flooded her eyes, and, rising, she threw herself into his arms.

"Oh, Tom —"

Rademacher held her close, endeavoring to soothe her while a towering rage ripped through him. Keck was everything low he'd figured the man to be — and he'd pay for what he'd done.

"It's all right now," he murmured as the girl continued to tremble against him.

The sobbing began to subside and after a time she drew back, wiped at her eyes. There were burned spots on her dress where sparks had fallen and soot streaked her face. He held her by the shoulders, looked at her closely.

"They hurt you or Rex any?"

"No. . . . Is the doctor coming?"

"Figured he'd be here ahead of me. Was gone when I got there. Had to take care of some woman having a baby."

Modesty lowered her glance to Rex. He lay perfectly still on his pad of quilts oblivious to what was going on around him. His skin, dry as parchment, was a dull, deep-seated red.

"I — I hope he comes soon."

"He will," Tom assured her, letting his eyes drift around the yard. The barn, the cabin into which he had moved, had not been touched. Only the ranchhouse.

"How long since Keck was here?"

"An hour, maybe two. I'm not sure. . . . It wasn't long after you drove off that they came."

116

"They were somewhere close at the time," he said. "Keck sent Hatton and Sackett and somebody they called Hank to follow me. Idea was to keep me from getting back. I managed to slip by them."

"I did what you said, locked up and stayed inside. I tried to stall Keck, too. It worked for a while, then they surrounded the house and started breaking down the doors. I used the shotgun a couple of times but it didn't do any good.

"They finally knocked in the kitchen door. Keck had two of them pick up Rex and carry him outside. Said he was going to burn the place down so we'd have to get off. I tried to talk to him but he wouldn't listen — it was like he'd gone crazy or something. When I saw it was no use, I took one of the quilts and made a pallet for Rex here in the yard.

"While I was doing that some of the men were pouring oil on everything and then started the fire to going. It took only a few minutes and then everything was burning. Everything — all we own."

Rademacher listened in silence as anger and hate continued to build within him. Before he had felt himself to be on the outside of the affair, an onlooker, doing what he could to help a girl who had aroused more than his casual interest, and her brother. He had been frank in his belief that they could not win against a man like Joe Keck, but he had listened to their hopes and admired their determination to the point where he had eventually been caught up and made a stand.

There was no doubt in his mind now that he was deeply involved. It was not in him to look the other way, ignore this latest attempt on the part of the rancher to force the Todds off their land. Destroying their house, their property was an unforgivable crime in a country where everything a man possessed he earned the hard way. Such applied not only to the Todds but to every other family settling the land.

And he had his own personal reason for calling out the rancher for a showdown. Keck had ordered him killed, and the three men sent to accomplish the fact had tried their best to do so. Keck would answer for that also.

"It didn't take long," the girl murmured. "The house burned in hardly any time at all. . . . When I think of all the years it took to make it what it was —"

"Shame, no missing that," he replied. "Main thing is you didn't get hurt — and a house can be rebuilt. Keck say anything to you before he left?"

"Said this settled it, that he'd be back at dark and we'd better be gone. Told me we could pick up the money he was giving us for the place, and sign the papers, at the bank when we got to town. I told him I couldn't move Rex. He just laughed and said it was my problem."

"That what you want to do now?"

Modesty glanced around forlornly. "There's nothing left. I can't see that there's anything else to do. . . . I decided that earlier. I had a feeling that he had done something to you, that you wouldn't come back — and there wasn't much use going on."

"He tried, but I'm here. . . . Far as losing everything, you've still got the cabin and the barn and the sheds. And you've got the land and your stock."

She stirred wearily. "There's no point in dragging it out. Sooner or later we'd have to give in. Like as not he'll set fire to all the rest if we're still here when he comes again."

"Probably try. Thing is, do you want to give up, take the money and call it quits?"

"No, but I can't fight him alone."

"You're not alone."

She turned to him, frowning. "But Rex can't —"

"Not meaning Rex. Was sort of standing by, helping before, mainly because I got my own problem and didn't want to get sidetracked. Figure now, after what Keck's done, that can wait another day or two. If you want to hang on, count me in all the way."

"But you said it was hopeless — useless!"

"Maybe it still is. I just ain't one to say but I do know I don't like letting Keck get away with it." Tom paused as a remnant of charred wall, still standing starkly upright, fell suddenly sending up a cloud of sparks and smoke. "Guess things happening like they have sort of changed me."

A glint of hope sprang into Modesty's eyes. It dulled quickly. "Just us, two of us — what could we do against Keck? At first I thought there was a chance but you see how it ended."

"Was my bad luck to be gone. Won't be that way again. And we've kind of got him running sideways — you and Rex bucking him like you've been doing and now me still walking around and breathing when I'm supposed to be dead. Going to jolt him no end when he finds that out."

"You've been hurt!" she exclaimed, noticing the bloody streak across his arm for the first time. "Let me get —" Her words broke off as she realized medicine, bandages and all such were lost in the fire with everything else.

"No matter, no more than a scratch," Rademacher said, and then added, "Need for you to decide what you want to do. If Keck's coming back at dark we sure want to be ready."

Modesty shook her head. "How — with everything gone —"

"Can move into the cabin, fort up there. Noticed there were a few pots and pans, enough to make do. And I brought all the stuff you wanted from the store." He didn't go into the problem of refused credit on the part of Kiefer and say that he had overcome it by paying for the purchase out of his own pocket. It would only serve to further upset her. "Plenty growing in your garden, and you've still got your chickens and such."

"But we couldn't hold out forever."

"Likely won't have to. He finds us all set and waiting for him, he'll be forced to make some kind of a move." Rademacher hesitated. A hardness had come into his voice when he continued. "An opening is all I need. We get rid of him, the trouble's over."

"But — but killing him, you'd never get the chance! Always keeps several of those gunmen with him so's it can't happen."

"There's a couple that won't be around," Tom said quietly. "That's going to start him thinking a bit."

"Still has a half a dozen others, and you can't fight them all."

"Man needs to do something, he finds a way."

The light had returned to Modesty's eyes but it was a different sort of glow, one now of softness and deep concern.

"I don't know, Tom. I'm afraid for you to try. If anything happened to you I'd never forgive myself — or ever forget, either. Nothing is worth your getting shot."

Rademacher smiled at her, masking his embarrassment. A practical, plain-minded man, he was always ill at ease where emotion was involved.

"Fretting over me's plumb foolish. I'm plenty good when it comes to dodging bullets."

Modesty turned from him, glanced down at her brother now stirring restlessly. "I know what Rex would want. He'd rather die than give in."

"It's what you want I'm waiting to hear. If you say quit, then that's how it'll be. We'll wait until the doc comes and fixes him up, then I'll move you both into town — and I'll see that you get your money.

"But if you say we stay, then that's it. We'll fight Keck the only way he savvys, with bullets, and we'll keep at it until it's finished, one way or the other."

She faced him soberly. "Tell me this, Tom,

will it be because you've found somebody else to hate, somebody besides the man that killed your brother, or will it be because of me? I — I've got to know."

He realized he hadn't given Virgil or Gabe Claunch much thought in those past hours, and it surprised him. But nothing had really changed; Virgil was still dead and Claunch had to be made to pay.

"What I'm doing, I'm doing for you."

Tears suddenly filled the girl's eyes. Turning, she threw her arms about him once again.

"I hoped you'd say that, Tom. Hoped — and prayed. I was afraid before but now that's gone. Nothing matters as long as you're here with me."

Chapter 16

For a long minute they stood there in the smoke haze that had settled over the yard, a slender woman, a tall, lonely man with too much of his life wasted and behind him. Finally he spoke, his voice remote, his words alien to the moment.

"Reckon you'd best get a bed fixed for Rex. I'll bring him in."

Modesty drew back searching his stolid features wonderingly as if she had expected different from him. Abruptly she turned, started for the cabin. Rademacher stepped to Todd's side woodenly. Kneeling, he slipped his thick arms under the pallet and rose, lifting the wounded man with ease. Coming about, he carried him as he might a child to the quarters once occupied by the family.

Modesty had cleared off the bed in a room not being used by Tom and was waiting silently in the doorway. Laying Rex down gently on the husk filled pad, Rademacher immediately pulled away.

"I'll be toting in the supplies," he said and returned to the yard.

Crossing to the buckboard he loaded the articles scattered around in the bed into the boxes Kiefer had placed them in, deposited the containers on the kitchen table and then led the worn little gray to the barn. Stabling the horse, he rolled the buckboard to the front of the cabin and capsized it, as he had done earlier with the wagon.

Pausing then to organize his thoughts, he began prowling about the sheds and barn until he found two serviceable casks that would do for water. Filling each near full at the pump, he cant-rolled them to the cabin where he stationed one in the kitchen and the other just inside the front door. It was a repeat of precautions previously taken but it had to be done.

Modesty, quiet and expressionless, was busy storing the supplies on shelves and taking stock of her cooking utensils and other necessary equipment. At his question concerning such she told him there wasn't much to work with but that she'd make out.

"Got a feeling it'll only be for today," he said, pausing near the door. "Ought to be over with by sunup."

"Tomorrow," she echoed, almost indifferently. "One way or the other it'll be done with."

Her tone was not lost to him. After a bit

he shrugged, said, "I'll get you some firewood. There anything else you're needing?"

The girl shook her head. "I'll look after the chickens, and getting things from the garden. You go ahead with what you have to do."

He moved on, going first to the barn, his mind now occupied with the serious matter of preparing to make a stand against Joe Keck and a half a dozen or more of his hardcase followers. He had but two weapons to depend on, his six-gun and rifle, he realized; all others had been lost in the fire, but he did have a good supply of ammunition, thanks to the purchase made at Kiefer's.

With more weapons it would be wise to place them about in convenient spots, thus make it possible to move around and cover the premises from many points, but that was out now. He was forced to concentrate his fire power at one position — the cabin itself. He didn't like the idea much since it meant subjecting Modesty and Rex to a considerable amount of danger, but it was best under the circumstances.

By the same token it would be smart to eliminate as many hiding places available to Keck and his men as possible. Accordingly, he made a close inspection of the barn, closing all windows, blocking openings and barring the rear doors. He was unable to secure the front entrance except from the outside and with a length of wire. It was no great worry, however, since anyone attempting to enter the structure would be visible and under his gunsight at all times.

There was little he could do about the remaining sheds and corrals but since they were not conveniently adjacent to the cabin, Keck would be unable to make any good use of them other then setting them afire. That was the one thing he must constantly be on the alert for, fire, and certainly the torch would again be a weapon the rancher would rely heavily upon.

Undoubtedly Keck would attempt to keep everyone inside the cabin busy with part of his force while he sent others with burning brands to start fires along its walls. That would be Modesty's job, Tom decided, keeping a sharp lookout and warning him when such attempts were being made so that he could turn his gun to stopping them.

It was like the old days, he thought, times when people prepared for an Indian attack; but that was something that seldom occurred any more. Trouble now came from greedy white men seeking to increase their wealth.

Leaving the barn, Rademacher crossed to the cabin and began kicking away any trash and brush that had blown up against its walls.

There was a considerable amount piled up on the west side, and giving it consideration, he collected it all a safe distance from the structure and put a match to it, adding to the roaring flames the rest of the dry growth that lay nearby.

The crackling fire brought Modesty hurriedly into the open to see what was taking place. He noticed the anxiety on her features, realized he had given her a bad scare.

"Guess I wasn't thinking good," he said, apologizing.

Her distant attitude appeared to have softened somewhat. She smiled, shook her head. "I should have known — but for a bit I was afraid Keck had come back and slipped up on you."

"Just fixing it so it's not so easy to burn down the house if he takes the notion to try again. You making out all right inside?"

The girl nodded, looked off toward the road. "I wish the doctor would come. Rex seems so weak and I'm sure his fever is worse."

"Ought to be showing up soon. His wife figured he'd get here before I made the trip back from town. I guess that baby was late."

She shrugged, signifying her agreement. Then, "Do you need any help out here? I've done all I can inside."

Tom glanced around. As the minutes of the day dragged by tension was gradually increasing and he knew she needed something to fill her mind, take it off the coming confrontation.

"Trying to pick up all the pieces of wood and such that Keck could use for torches and get them out of the way," he said. "You want to lend a hand at that I'll be obliged."

Modesty moved off at once, using her apron as a basket into which she dropped the dead branches, bits of combustible items that were scattered about the yard. The lack of tinder would serve to delay Joe Keck and his men only briefly, Tom knew; there was plenty of fuel for such a short distance from the cabin and they had only to go there for their needs. But nothing would be handy and creating the delay could only be of help.

The chore finally completed, both started back for the cabin, Rademacher sweeping the hardpack and buildings with his glance for a final time. He had done all he could think of toward shifting the advantage to their favor and thus reduce the odds they would be facing. What happened next, when Keck and his men arrived would depend on luck and his own skill with weapons.

"Someone's coming —"

He heard the solid thud of a loping horse at the same moment that Modesty did. At once he pushed her toward the cabin, urging her into a run.

"They're early," he said tautly. "When we get inside, you see to the doors while I get set at the window."

They reached the rear of the house, entered. Rademacher hurried to the front, hearing the dull sound of the bar being dropped into its brackets behind him as the girl secured the door. She passed close by him as she crossed the room to also safeguard the forward entrance. Crowding up to the window, he threw his glance toward the road beyond the burned remains of the ranchhouse. A lone rider was just rounding the still smoking embers.

"Hello, the Todds!"

A gasp of relief escaped Modesty's lips. "It's the doctor!" she cried, and hastily opened the door.

Chapter 17

Rademacher holstered his pistol, followed the girl into the open. Ross, a sandy looking man with piercing blue eyes, was dressed in a drab gray suit over which he had pulled a duster, a narrow-brimmed hat and ordinary button shoes. He was astride a barrel-bodied little buckskin that looked as if he would be more at home pulling a plow.

The physician bobbed his head, said, "Modesty," in greeting and swung stiffly off his mount. Glancing about he added, "Been a long time since I sat leather making a call. Left my buggy at the Carvers' and borrowed Abe's horse so's I could get here faster. . . . What happened to the house?"

"Joe Keck," Modesty replied.

Ross said, "Him again, eh," and shook his head. "Where's the patient?"

"In here," the girl said, pointing at the cabin. "We've moved back into it."

Rademacher felt the physician's sharp glance cover him as he passed, raking him from head to toe, making an assessment. He returned the look candidly, fell in behind the man and trailed him and Modesty into the house, halting just inside the doorway.

Ross stepped into the bedroom where Todd lay. Almost at once he said, "I'll be needing hot water and some clean cloth."

The girl hurried to the kitchen, her face drawn with worry. Evidently she had anticipated the doctor's needs, had a kettle simmering on the stove. Taking up the container and grabbing a shallow pan from a shelf, she returned to the bedroom.

"There are no clean cloths, doctor. We lost about everything we had in the fire."

"Never mind. I've got enough gauze and cotton with me. Now, you wait in the other room. I'll call out if I need you."

Modesty drew back. "Is he bad off?"

"Bad enough," Ross answered gruffly. "You waited too long to call me, but that's usually the way of it. Folks always hold off until the last minute for some reason."

"Rex wouldn't let me. I wanted to but he kept saying he'd be all right." The girl's voice broke. "He will, won't he?"

The physician's voice was muffled as he bent over his patient. "Probably. We'll see."

Modesty turned disconsolately into the room. She noticed Rademacher leaning against the door frame, changed course and moved toward him. He extended a hand to her but she ignored it, paused nearby.

"Rex'll come out of it," Rademacher said, hoping to cheer her. "I've seen men shot up worse than him that lived to talk about it."

She merely nodded, stared out across the yard, past the charred house to the rolling land beyond. Todd's voice came to them, faintly protesting and over-ridden by Ross's deeper tones. Finally the medical man was finished with his ministrations. Modesty wheeled anxiously to him as he came from the bedroom.

"Will he be all right?" she asked.

"Near as I can tell," Ross replied, setting his satchel on the kitchen table. He began to rummage around inside it, produced a bottle of pills. Pouring out a handful, he gave them to the girl.

"Feed him one of these every three hours until the fever's gone. I'll look in again on him tomorrow. You should have brought him to me right after it happened."

"I wanted to —"

"I know. Rex always was a stubborn one. Was sorry to hear about John."

At her surprised look, he ducked his head at Tom. "Your friend, there. He told my wife and she passed it on to the hired man. He gave me the story when she sent him to the Carvers'." Abruptly the physician pivoted to Rademacher, extended his hand. "Since we haven't met officially, I'm Pike Ross."

"Tom Rademacher."

"Pleased to know you, and glad you were around to give this girl some help. She's had a hard time of it."

"Wishing now I could've got here sooner the other day. Things might've turned out different for her."

"You weren't here?"

Rademacher jerked a thumb toward the ridge to the north of the yard. "Was up there. Rode down fast as I could when the shooting started."

Ross bobbed his head slowly, began to close his bag. "What brought it on?"

"Keck's still after us to sell out, let him have the ranch. Rode in that morning with several of his men. When John refused to listen to him he took out his pistol and started shooting out the windows of the house. John and Rex had their guns, too. They started to use them. Keck's men began to shoot then. John was killed right away. Rex was wounded."

Modesty's voice sounded far away, her words almost beyond hearing. Ross seemed not to notice her reluctance or else, believing it best she speak of it, pressed on.

"Then they came back this morning, set fire to the place —"

"This was the second time since the

shooting. Tom was here before and drove them off, but this morning he'd gone to town after you."

"I see. . . . Keck seems never to give up. What are you going to do now, with John gone?"

"We haven't changed. We intend to stay."

Ross glanced around the barren room. "Is it worthwhile? The fire has cost you about everything, and alone —"

"I'm not alone. Tom is staying — at least until it's over."

"Until it's over." Ross repeated the words thoughtfully. "Expect you know that killing Joe Keck is the only way that'll come to pass."

"We know," Rademacher said, "and we can use some help. It's a bit late to talk about it but it's high time your town was waking up to what's going on here in the valley. Not right to let a man like him run loose, get away with whatever he wants."

"Agreed," Ross said, "but getting someone to take a stand is a problem."

"They've got a good reason now. John Todd's been shot down and Rex bad hurt. On top of that the ranchhouse has been burned to the ground. Too late to help the other folks Keck's tramped on but they could sure do something for the Todds."

Ross, chewing on his lower lip, continued to stare out the window.

"How about doing a little talking when you get back to town?" Rademacher suggested. "We don't look for Keck to show up until dark. There'll be time enough to get a posse together and on the way here."

The physician stirred, shrugged. "I wouldn't count on it. First place I'm in the middle, neutral. My job's to look after everybody no matter who they are and what side of the fence they're on."

"Man can't be in the middle at a time like this. Either he's for right or he's not. Same goes for the rest of the people in your town. If they don't make a stand against Keck he'll soon have them squirming under his heel. You ought to be able to see that."

"I suppose I do," Ross said. "And I guess there are a few more around that recognize the possibility but they're not apt to do anything about it."

"Why not? It's their town — their neck."

"Mainly because nobody yet has been able to buck Joe Keck and his gang of gunslingers. They figure they wouldn't have a chance against them — and they have too much to lose."

"Going to wake up someday and find out they've lost it anyway. They make a move now they'll at least be putting up a fight for what they've got."

Ross, arms folded across his chest, was again staring through the window but his eyes now were on the blackened remains of the Todd house. The calmness with which the man had accepted the disaster that had struck Modesty and her brothers had surprised Tom. Instead of showing anger and indignation, he appeared to view it as if it were an unavoidable occurrence, an act of nature such as a tornado or a flooding river.

"You're right, of course," the physician said finally, "but I don't know what can be done about it."

"Can tell you easy," Rademacher said harshly. "Get a few of the men in your town together and be back here by dark — with guns. We don't intend to let Keck run us off and a little outside help will not only make it easier for us but it'll show Keck that his day's come — that he's through doing whatever he wants.

"When a man like him gets no opposition, it works on him like a disease. He quick gets the idea that he can pull anything no matter how raw it is. Now's the time to let him know different — and an armed posse can be mighty convincing."

Ross was quiet for a long minute after

Rademacher had finished. Then, "Well, I can try —"

"Will you?" Modesty cried, suddenly hopeful. "Oh, doctor, if only you could!"

"Can't promise much, maybe nothing at all. But like your friend there says it's high time something was done about Joe Keck, and if the two of you have the courage to stand up against him, maybe I can shame some of the men in town into lining up beside you."

"Can tell them like as not, once they make a show, there won't be any shooting — or killing."

"I'll talk my best," Ross said, picking up his bag and closing it with a snap.

"All we ask," Rademacher said, but there was no real enthusiasm behind his words. Too many times he had seen a situation of like nature and almost always those parties involved had been forced to meet their crisis without help. It was to be expected; most people, burdened with their own problems, had no heart for taking on someone else's even if it did affect them. But it was worth trying for.

Ross, satchel under his arm, moved to the doorway and stepped out into the bright sunshine. "I'll head straight back to town, get my buggy later. That will let me get busy at recruiting sooner."

He smiled at his bit of humor as Modesty and Tom followed him across the yard to the buckskin and waited while he climbed onto the saddle.

"Bones old as mine shouldn't be subjected to this kind of punishment," the physician mumbled, settling himself in the leather. Pulling his hat lower on his head, he leaned forward. "Now, I'll say it again, I'm not promising anything. I'll do what I can but I can't force anybody to come out here. Can only tell them what's going on, try to make them see it's their fight, too."

"Up to them," Tom said.

"Exactly," Ross agreed, and leaning over, shook first Modesty's hand and then Rademacher's. "However it goes, good luck — and don't forget to give Rex that medicine."

"I won't," the girl called after him as he wheeled about and started for the road.

She turned at once to Tom, eyes aglow with new hope. "Maybe they'll come. Maybe it won't have to end in shooting."

His shoulders stirred. "Could be, but we won't go planning on it. Even if he does talk a few of them into doing something, it's likely they won't get here in time to do us any good — unless they hurry. And a man thinking he's got a good chance of dying never gets in much of a rush."

"But they could, and if we can hold Keck off until they get here —"

"What we'll try to do."

Modesty nodded, and then abruptly she changed to a different matter. "Tom, when it's over, do you still plan to ride on, hunt for that man who killed your brother?"

"No choice," he answered. "Claunch has to be made to pay."

A small, hopeless sound slipped from her throat and she turned away quickly, started back for the cabin. Rademacher followed, halted when she hesitated in the doorway. She had recovered her composure as she faced him.

"Have you got everything fixed the way you planned?"

"Much as I could."

"Then there's nothing to do but wait."

"About covers it. We just sit and watch the road, see who shows up first — Keck or a posse from town."

There was little doubt in Tom Rademacher's mind as to the answer, and later as he hunched in the doorway listening to Modesty moving about in the kitchen preparing the evening meal while the shadows steadily lengthened, he saw that he was right.

Eight riders appeared at the edge of the

trees to the east of the ranch. The man in the lead, astride a nervous white horse could only be Joe Keck.

Chapter 18

Rising quickly Tom closed the door, dropped the bar into place, and glancing about to see that all else was secure, picked up his rifle.

"Keck's here," he said quietly.

Modesty uttered a small cry, whirled, rushed to the window where Rademacher had taken a stand. It was much the same crowd of hardcases the rancher had brought with him before except for Sackett and the one called Hank — both missing for good reason. All lined up behind Keck as if engaged in some sort of cavalry drill exercise, and then as the rancher roweled the big white lightly, they moved forward.

Tom's eyes fastened on the rider in the center of the group. It was Webber. He was slumped forward on the saddle, hat pulled low over his eyes to shade them from the last glare of the sun and again denying Rademacher a good look at the man. But he was present and that brought a grimness to Tom; this time he would find out for sure if he was or was not Gabe Claunch.

Stepping back to the table pulled into the

front area of the room, Rademacher ripped open the two boxes of cartridges he'd purchased and dumped their contents into separate piles where the bullets would be readily accessible.

"Still coming?" he asked, without glancing up.

Modesty's voice sounded strained in the warm hush of the cabin. "They're alongside the house — what's left of it. . . . I don't think they know where we are."

"About time they found out," he said, returning to the window. Raising it slightly, he balanced the barrel of the rifle on the sill, drove a bullet into the ground only inches in front of the stallion's hooves.

The riders halted instantly. As the shot echoed about the yard Keck's horse reared, began to shy, walking on his hind legs like a circus performer. Swearing, jerking at the bit, the rancher struggled to bring his mount under control. The party had moved past the blackened scar that had been the Todd ranchhouse, were now near the center of the hardpack that separated it from the cabin.

The men from town — they didn't come.

At Modesty's forlorn words Rademacher shrugged. "Wasn't much looking for them. Most folks believe in others skinning their own snakes and figure to do the same for themselves."

"But Dr. Ross said —"

"Only said he'd try." Reaching for the window, Tom raised it a bit higher and leaned nearer to it. "You — Keck! You're as close as you'll get. Turn around and pull out if you want to stay alive."

The rancher holding to the reins of the white with his left hand, patting the neck of the still fractious horse with the right, glanced at the riders strung out on either side. He said something, laughed. The men joined in. Webber, brushing his hat to the back of his head, scrubbed at the stubble on his jaw. Tom studied the man intently. It could be Claunch but he just wasn't sure.

"Rademacher — that you?"

"It's me, and I'm standing here with my rifle lined up on your head. Was I thinking straight I'd blow you off that horse right now for what you've done to the Todds but I figure there's been enough killing so I'm letting it pass."

"*You're* letting it pass!" Keck repeated with fine scorn. "Mister, you ain't in no shape to do nothing but come marching out of that shack with your hands over your head — you and them Todds!"

"No deal. They don't want to give up the place."

"Then I reckon I'll just have to move you out."

"Up to you. Trying's going to spill some blood and it'll start with yours."

Keck appeared to give that thought, and then motioning to his men, swung about. In single file they followed him to the opposite side of the burned house.

Rademacher watched narrowly, not certain what the rancher had in mind. He would like to believe Keck had taken him at his word and was calling it off, but he had doubts. The man would not give up that easily.

"What are they going to do?" Modesty wondered.

Tom shook his head. The moments when he had them all under the muzzle of his rifle were gone. He swore silently, chiding himself for not making the most of the opportunity; certainly had the situation been reversed Joe Keck would have granted him no such consideration. But he knew even as he gave it thought that he could not have done it. Killing a man in a shootout was one thing, cold blooded murder was something else and no part of him.

"You want to let the girl come out?"

Keck, voicing his question from behind the

heat withered shrubbery beyond the charred house, was not visible.

"Ain't got it in mind to hurt her none — just want her gone. Quarrel's with you now. Cut yourself in on this game, shot up a couple of my boys. I don't let nobody get away with that. Send her out and I'll let her head for town. . . . Don't reckon it makes much difference about Rex."

Tom looked questioningly at Modesty. Lips set to a stubborn line, she said, "No."

"Might be smart —"

"I'll not go," she declared flatly. "Never. Whatever happens, happens to us all."

Rademacher again faced the partly open window. "Forget it, Keck."

There was no response from the rancher, and silence could mean only one thing — he was preparing to make his move. Grim, Tom nodded to the girl.

"They're getting ready. Want you to keep low and stay back from the windows. Shutters are heavy enough to stop a bullet but they might get lucky and put one clean through."

The stubbornness was in her eyes again. "I'll watch for them trying to start fires, like you said. . . . And I can use that rifle."

"All right, if it comes down to it, but I figure I can do pretty good from here unless they split up and get around back."

Such, he decided, would undoubtedly be Keck's plan; men moving in from all four sides. It was about the only way the rancher could hope to force them into the open. Just how long he could keep Crosshatch at bay, prevent them from getting in near enough to start the walls of the cabin blazing, was anybody's guess.

Hell, he'd gone about it all wrong. . . . It would have been better to hole up in the barn and thereby be in a position to keep them away from the cabin. Rademacher shrugged off his second-guessing; that wouldn't have worked too well, either. He wouldn't have been able to see the south wall. Keck would have noticed that at once and centered his attention upon it.

The answer was to stop them before they could split up, not permit them to start circling. He rolled that about in his mind, came to a decision. The risk wouldn't be too great since the buckboard shielding the door would provide fair cover if he kept moving fast.

Hanging the rifle in the crook of his arm, he turned to the table and grabbed up a handful of the spare cartridges. Stuffing them into a pocket, he swung to the door.

Modesty had been watching him closely. "What are you going to do?" she asked, alarm filling her voice.

"See if I can stop them before they start," he said, lifting the bar. "Soon as I'm outside, put this back in place."

She was staring at him, eyes wide with fear and concern. "You mean you're going out there?"

He bucked his head, opened the thick panel a narrow crack and peered through. Keck and the others were still behind the ruined ranchhouse, vague shadows in the thin screen of smoke and closing darkness. Half turning, Rademacher grinned at the girl.

"No big problem. Aim to keep the buckboard between them and me. . . . Ready?"

She moved quickly to him. "No, Tom, I won't let you!"

"Afraid it's the only chance we've got," he said, and hunching, pulled back the door and darted through.

The overturned vehicle was only steps away. Within the space of a breath he was in behind it, crouched low. At once he heard the door close, the dull thump of the bar dropping into place. He grunted in relief. Modesty had obeyed, not tried to call him back, or worse, follow him.

He shifted his attention to the yonder side of the ranchhouse. The riders were beginning to move. He could see the indefinite shapes of some moving to the left, others to the right.

A faint blur of white indicated that Keck was staying in the center. Likely he would wait until his men had reached positions around the cabin, and then with two or three picked gunmen at his side for protection, would move directly in from the front.

"You got yourself a surprise coming, friend," Rademacher muttered, and hitching his way to the extreme left end of the buckboard, cocked the hammer of his rifle.

Chapter 19

Rising suddenly, Rademacher leveled the rifle, sighted, pressed off a shot. The first of the two riders on his left yelled, sagged in the saddle. Tom pivoted, snapped a bullet at the pair moving out from the opposite end of the ranchhouse. His aim was true. The man jolted, clawed at his arm. Wheeling, he spurred back toward Keck, his companion following equally fast.

Again hunched behind the buckboard, Rademacher waited. He had halted Keck's plans for surrounding the house, but only temporarily. The rancher and his gang would try again — this time with less disdain for his presence, however.

The delay was short-lived. Abruptly guns began to blast. Bullets thudded into the bed of the buckboard, splintered wood, caromed off metal. Yells went up and then Tom heard the quick hammer of running horses. They were rushing him under cover of a hail of lead.

Cool, knowing he had little chance and that the odds now for staying alive were about equal whether he kept low or stood and fought, Rademacher drew himself upright to gain a better sweep of the yard. Four men were driving in on him, two from each side. The others, still beyond the ranchhouse, were affording the blanket of bullets.

He fired hastily at the rider nearest on his left, missed. Levering a fresh cartridge into the chamber, ignoring the storm of bullets, he tried again. The man wilted, swung away. Again jacking the carbine, Tom threw a shot at the second rider, and without waiting to see if he'd scored, spun hurriedly as he reloaded and triggered lead at the two bearing in on his opposite flank and almost abreast the buckboard.

His shot knocked the man from his saddle, but the rider with him, veered sharply, pounded on by. Rademacher squatted, swore deeply as he fed cartridges into the magazine of the weapon. He'd failed in keeping Keck's gunmen from getting past him; now there was one, possibly two, if the second rider on the left had not turned back, in behind him and on the rear side of the cabin. They'd lose no time quitting their saddles and working their way in on him while Keck and the rest kept him busy from the front.

The shooting slowed, fell off altogether. Tom braced himself. The squeeze was about to begin — one, maybe two guns pressing in from the back, Keck and the others crowding in head-on from the yard. He was in a vise, and soon to be caught in a wicked crossfire. Taut, he checked the rifle, drew his pistol and laid it on the edge of the buckboard's bed where it would be handy.

A realist, Tom Rademacher had no illusions regarding his chances of surviving such an assault, and if it was the way it was all to end, let it. One thing was certain, however, he'd see to it that Joe Keck and a couple of the others went down with him. He'd not die before he did that much for Modesty Todd — and for the rest of the people in the Sage River Valley whether they deserved it or not.

Crouched in the semi-darkness, he shrugged. Folks were a funny lot sometimes — most of the time, in fact. They hated Joe Keck for what he had done and was doing, knew deep inside them that he was their enemy and one day would have to be reckoned with, yet they held off, reluctant to make a move toward stopping him.

Small rattlesnakes grew and became large and deadly. The time to end danger from them was when they could still be handled. The Sage Valley people had overlooked that, permitted Joe Keck to grow in size and strength until he became capable of forcing his will and ruthless ways upon others unopposed. They could have still put an end to it if they'd listened to Doc Ross and pitched in to help — but they had not, and that was what he'd expected.

Now it was up to him alone, and before it was done with, a lot of blood would be spilled — his included. But, thinking of Modesty, he guessed it wouldn't be too high a price to pay; at least he would be bringing an end to her troubles.

Suddenly Keck and those with him opened up again. Once more bullets began to thunk into the thick floor of the buckboard, scream off the iron tires and braces, thud into the walls of the cabin behind him and shatter the glass in the windows.

Rademacher rolled to the end of the vehicle, fired once to establish his position for the attackers, now only dim shapes off their horses and moving straight toward him in a forage line, and then crawled hurriedly to the opposite end of the buckboard's bed.

Chancing the man who would be slipping up along the wall of the cabin from its rear, he rose. Directly ahead through the drifting layers of gunsmoke, he could see Keck. There was a man siding the rancher on his left, two more on his right — one of them Pete Webber. They approached steadily, firing as they came, hoping to keep him pinned down by the sheer power of their guns.

A bullet slammed into Tom's shoulder, spun him half around. He caught the edge of the overturned wagon, steadied himself and triggered a shot at Keck. He saw the rancher stagger, go to his knees.

Shifting the carbine slightly, he pressed off his next bullet at Webber. The gunman came to a halt, his shoulders slumping forward. A lead slug caught the edge of the buckboard near Tom, showering his face and neck with splinters. He ignored the stinging pain, whipped a shot at the rider hesitating uncertainly near Webber. It was a near miss but the man whirled immediately, ran for the horses beyond the charred ranchhouse.

A thundering force smashed into Rademacher's leg, knocked him flat. The rifle clanked against the wheel of the buckboard, spun from his grasp. Down full length, he snatched up the pistol he'd laid close by, fired point-blank at a dark figure coming at him from the corner of the cabin. . . . The rider, or one of the riders, who'd gotten in behind him. The looming shape lurched back, disappeared.

Pain roaring through him, Rademacher twisted about. The remaining man should be making his play, assuming there was another.

And there had been three gunnies siding Keck in the yard which meant there was still one in front of him to be accounted for. He stiffened, hearing the door of the cabin open. Modesty, her features torn with anxiety, looked down at him.

"Get back!" he yelled. "Not over yet!"

She seemed not to hear, simply stood there, eyes spread with fear, lips parted as if she were trying to speak but found it impossible. Tom struggled to a sitting position. His leg was numb, refused to respond, and there was no strength in his arm. . . . If he could manage to get on his feet —

"No, Lon — no!"

Modesty's scream cut through him like a knife. He jerked around. Phillips was only a stride away, pistol leveled. There *had* been two of Keck's men get by him and reach the yard behind the cabin during that first rush. Lon Phillips had been one of them — and Phillips now had him cold. The tall rider had but to press the trigger of the weapon in his hand and it would be all over.

For what seemed an eternity Lon hung there poised, motionless, and then with a fleeting, lost look at Modesty, he stepped back into the shadows beyond the buckboard. Holstering his gun, he wheeled, strode hurriedly toward the horses.

Soaked with sweat, pain jabbing mercilessly through him, Rademacher reached for the edge of the buckboard, struggled to pull himself upright. In his mind's eye he was seeing Lon Phillips standing over him, recalling again the nearness of death, realizing, also, that it had been Modesty's scream that had stayed the rider's hand.

Abruptly the girl was beside him, sobbing uncontrollably as she helped him to his feet.

"I'm doing fine," he mumbled.

He couldn't make out what she was saying. Words were tumbling from her lips in an unintelligible torrent. Steadying himself against the bullet pocked bed of the vehicle, he looked at the two figures lying almost side by side in the center of the yard.

"Is — is that —"

He understood her then. "Yeh, one's Keck. He won't be giving you or anybody else trouble from now on." Pausing for a moment, he added: "Other's the one who called himself Webber. Be obliged if you'll help me —"

"You're hurt bad — shot!" Modesty protested. "I'll find something for bandages, stop the bleeding —"

"I'm not dying, and I've got to see if that's who he really is. I'm thinking maybe — hoping —"

Tom let the words dwindle away. The girl pressed up beside him, placed his uninjured arm around her shoulders, and together they moved out from behind the buckboard and crossed to where the two men lay.

Halting beside Webber, Rademacher looked down at the gunman's slack, placid features. Stirring wearily, he shook his head.

"He's not Gabe Claunch."

Chapter 20

Modesty moaned softly, tightened her arm around his waist.

"I'm wishing it was," he said, and looked off toward the road as the rapid thump of a trotting horse and the grating sound of wheels cutting into the soil drew his attention. Moments later Ross, alone in his buggy, wheeled into the yard, pulled to a stop.

The physician dropped to the ground, glanced around hurriedly and crossed to where Tom and the girl stood.

"God in heaven!" he murmured. "Place looks like a battlefield. Glad to see you're both still alive. I tried to get you some help. Nobody'd listen. . . . You shot up bad?"

"Seen worse," Rademacher replied, and lowering his gaze, fell to studying Webber once more.

Ross looked at him curiously. "There something special about that one? He was just another of Keck's hired killers."

"Tom was hoping he'd be the man he's been hunting for years — the one who killed his brother."

The physician's mouth sagged. "You say —
for years?"

The astonishment in the man's voice angered Tom. "That's right — years. Time's
got nothing to do with it. He shot my brother
— only a kid — killed him in cold blood.
I've been hunting him ever since, and I aim
to go on doing it until I've found him, made
him pay."

Ross shrugged. "Like as not he's already
paid."

"Paid — how?"

"Killers like him eventually have to face
their own Armageddon. They never escape
it. Maybe they get by for a while but sooner
or later some good man comes along and gives
them their just dues. My guess would be that
this murderer you're after is dead and buried
somewhere by now."

Tom gave that thought, shook his head.
"Like to believe that, but there's no way of
knowing for sure."

"No? You're proof of what I'm saying,
yourself. We had Joe Keck around here,
running rough-shod over everybody and
anybody. Then you show up and put a stop
to it. . . . Like I said, a good man always
comes along, sets things right. Now, let's get
inside where there's some light so's I can fix
you up."

Rademacher felt Modesty's arm tighten about his middle again as he turned slowly for the cabin. Her voice was low and filled with hope when she spoke.

"Tom, the doctor's right about Claunch. I'm sure of it."

"So am I," he replied, and smiling, drew her closer.